Also by J

Lane's End

Un-Stable Lane

The Third Lane

A Bend in the Lane

Never Run Away

Never Pretend

A Lesson for the Teacher

More Fish in the Sea

Julie C. Round

Published by New Generation Publishing in 2020

Copyright © Julie C. Round 2020

First Edition

ISBN: 978-1-80031-933-2

www.newgeneration-publishing.com

New Generation Publishing

To Tracy

Prologue

There was a "whoop," a splash – and then silence.

Matt looked down from the cliff top.

"I don't think...." came a voice behind him.

"I know," Matt interrupted. "That didn't sound right. He should have gone into the water where you did. Get down there, quick. We need to get him out."

The two men scrambled down the rocks and grabbed the floating body, hauling it onto the tiny beach.

"Your phone, Kenny," shouted Matt. "I'll try CPR. Call 999."

"It's no use," said Kenny. "Look at his face, look at his legs and look at the sea."

The surface of the sea was red, James's legs were crushed and twisted and his face was white, with a bloody gash on his forehead.

"No," yelled Matt, "He can't be."

"He is," responded Kenny. "He's dead."

When they told James's wife what had happened she screamed and screamed until they thought she would never stop.

"Show me," she gasped at last. "Show me where it happened," and they drove her to Cornwall and let her see the little rocky cove.

She stood on the cliff top and breathed in the salty air.

She was alone, now, no longer one of a pair. She had a funeral to arrange, people to contact, work to return to, a life to continue, but a life without the man she had thought she would grow old with.

She felt as if part of her had closed down. She would function – but her world had shrunk. She felt cold and wondered if she would ever be warm again.

Chapter 1

The front door seemed to echo as Valerie closed it and shook off her coat. The house was so empty without James.

She'd got through the anniversary of his death but still felt tempted to have a martini when she returned from work. Instead, she went into the kitchen and filled the kettle.

"I actually did it," she said out loud. "I made the appointment. It's probably a mistake but I have to think about the future, don't I?"

She felt the need to justify her actions. "A year is long enough to mourn, isn't it? I'll never forget him but I would like the opportunity to start a family. I never thought I would go to an introduction agency." Waiting for the voice in her head to challenge her decision she heard nothing.

"I certainly wouldn't do it on line. I'm going to make sure I know who I'm dealing with. They seemed very professional although I do feel I'm coping quite well on my own."

She was lucky, she supposed, that she had this little end terraced house by the coast but it was still quite exhausting to be travelling up to London and back for work five days a week.

She had considered looking for something closer but all the large stores were closing down, not taking on more staff. "I'm management," she had explained to anyone who asked. "Shops can't afford to employ me. They just promote someone from within and then take on a junior."

She had a quiet evening in front of the TV. Her favourite gardening programme was on and she promised herself she would visit the garden centre soon.

Two days later she had a text message from 'Ocean Introductions.' *We have two possibilities. Shall we email details or will you come in?*

I'll be in at 10am on Saturday, she responded. They know I don't want to do anything on line, she thought, remembering the form she had filled in, the photograph from the Summer Fayre she had supplied, because it was the happiest picture of herself she could find, and the hobbies she had indicated, gardening and reading. It didn't sound very exciting. Maybe she should have added swimming. Still, she would see what happened on Saturday.

Fiona Baker had a large shiny blue file in front of her on the desk.

"Tell me about yourself," she asked. "Filling in a form never really gives a true picture of a person. We always do in depth interviews. We have learned over time what questions to ask. It helps to weed out people who are not being honest. So many clients try too hard to make an impression."

It was such a relief to talk to someone new that Valerie found herself telling Fiona much more than she needed to know.

"I'm not very impressive. I thought I was settled for life. I had a house by the sea, a husband I loved, a job in London and a passion for gardens. It seemed enough until the accident."

"Tell me about it," Fiona encouraged, so Valerie did.

"James had gone on a stag weekend. I think they went co-steering. Anyway, they were climbing and swimming and jumping into the sea. James jumped where it was too shallow and fell onto rocks. He died almost instantly. The others got him out of the water and called the coastguard but it was too late to save him. His friend Kenny's wedding went ahead but my life was destroyed. It has taken over a year to begin to plan for a future without him. I'm still in the same house and with the same job but it's very lonely. We had so much in common. We had a fair sized allotment that we worked on together. James said it brought out my nurturing side."

"You didn't have children?"

"No. It just didn't happen. I suppose that's a good thing, now."

"Would you have liked a family?"

"I'm not sure. I thought I didn't care but now I'm beginning to wish we had explored the medical side. We weren't taking precautions."

"In your late thirties you are still young enough to start a family," Fiona said. "I've downloaded details of both men who asked to meet you. Would you like to look at them now?"

"Yes, please," Valerie replied. "I'm curious to know who would be interested in me."

"We have interviewed both applicants personally. One has seen a couple of other ladies without success. The other is new to our books."

"And they live locally?"

"Both live in Sussex. One lives in the city and the other further inland. If you are interested we have extra details which are confidential at this stage."

Valerie took the file and sat on a leather sofa in the corner of the office. The first photograph was a little disappointing, no George Clooney, instead, a thin faced man with dark rimmed spectacles wearing a collar and tie. It looked rather like a passport photo, although there was the hint of a shy smile.

He'll be a clerk, she thought, but she was wrong. He was a wine grower from Mid Sussex. It seemed grapes had been his passion for all his adult life and, at 39, he suddenly realised he was missing something and had enrolled with "Ocean Introductions."

Valerie turned to the next photograph. This was a more professional picture – more Cary Grant, dark haired and handsome. Valerie wondered why he was without a partner. She read the resume´. He had been married. His wife had died fifteen months ago. They had two adult children. This was the man from Brighton and he was a police officer.

I think I'll try him first, she thought.

"Neither gentleman has given us permission to reveal an email address," said Fiona, "but once you have met it is up to you. At this stage all we do is arrange a meeting, somewhere public and Ocean Introductions do have arrangements with two local restaurants if our clients wish."

"No. I wouldn't want that," said Valerie. "I would expect the man to suggest somewhere and see if I agree."

"Fair enough. Who would you like to contact?"

"I'd like to meet this one," she said, indicating the policeman.

"Shall I give him your number?"

"Yes, please. He's the new one, isn't he?"

"Richard Stillman – yes, and what about Cyril Hunter?"

"He looks interesting, too. Maybe later. You've been a great help."

Valerie sat in the café with a ham and cheese baguette and a cup of coffee. Her heart was thumping.

Had she really done this? Had she asked for a date with a mystery man? It was years since she had been on a date. Did she have the right clothes? Should she try a new hairstyle? She'd forgotten to ask how tall he was. Her details would have revealed that she was five foot six with brown eyes and a good education but no experience of university. Would that be a help or a hindrance? Pull yourself together, girl. People are doing this all the time, she told herself. She'd get the shopping and go home and make her favourite meal, macaroni cheese. She might have a glass of cider – and finish off with apple crumble and custard. She was half way through a novel which should hold her attention until bedtime and, of course, she needed to weigh up all the pros and cons.

On the day of the date Valerie surveyed her reflection. Was her hair too short? She liked it neat for work but what if Richard liked unruly hair? He knew she was a brunette. He'd seen her photo, but she had a softer, wavy, style then. It was too late to worry. Today she was wearing pink, a polka dot dress, a pink jacket and her best shoes. It was sunny and she felt excited. There was something about his photograph that made her feel hopeful.

The date with Richard Stillman was to be in a local restaurant.

Valerie had specified lunch. Then she could always plead an afternoon engagement if she wasn't comfortable. Richard had said he was content as it was an area he had not worked in.

He was there before her, in a blazer and slacks, and he stood up to greet her.

"You picked a good table," she said, "away from the door," and then blushed as it made her seem embarrassed to be seen with him.

"I made sure the place didn't have loud music," he said. "I hope you don't mind British food."

"I don't usually eat much at lunchtime, but there's bound to be salads."

"Here." He handed her a menu. "I'm a burger guy myself, very boring."

"I'd like the scampi and salad, please," she said at last.

"And a drink?"

"This does seem rather special, perhaps a white wine?"

Richard went to the bar, told them her choices and ordered his burger and a pint of beer.

"How long have you..." they both began.

"You first," he grinned.

"I've lived here for ten years," she said. "Before that we lived in West London. My husband died eighteen months ago. I still haven't really got over it. You'd think the nights would be the worst but I miss him so much at meal times. We used to chat about our days. It isn't the same, eating alone."

"I know the feeling," he said. "The first Christmas was the worst – but I had two children to consider, both grown up, but they took losing their mother to cancer quite hard."

"We didn't have any children," Valerie said. "What do yours think about this?"

"Dating?" He laughed. "They said, be careful – don't find anyone who is after your money!"

"They don't mind?"

"They're good kids. They just want me to be happy."

"It's nice when people say that," Valerie mused, taking a sip of her wine.

They completed their meal with ice cream and she agreed to see him again.

"Perhaps a show?" he suggested. "What would you like?"

"There is a film I would like to see," she replied. "It's on for another fortnight."

"Let me guess, the musical?"

Valerie laughed. "Let's make it Saturday week." and they arranged to meet at 2.30.

Chapter 2

It had all passed in a blur and Valerie wasn't sure how she felt. She had almost got used to her present situation. Richard was OK, she thought. Still, I'll give the other man a chance. I rather fancy a trip to a vineyard.

When Cyril Hunter rang next day he sounded rather hesitant, as if he was ready for a rejection. "Ocean Introductions gave me your number," he said. "Would it be possible to meet?"

"Where do you suggest, Cyril?" Valerie asked, feeling sorry for him already.

"Could you come to the vineyard? I'd pay for a taxi, or have you a car? The buses are not very frequent."

"I'd love to see where you work," she replied. "If you give me directions I'll arrange a taxi from this end. Then I'll be certain to get one back."

"Could you come on Sunday?" Cyril asked, "If it's not inconvenient."

She was beginning to feel this would be a disaster but it would be rude to back out now.

"What time would you like me to come?"

"About eleven? If the weather is OK I can show you round. Valerie, isn't it?"

"Yes, Valerie Davies. I look forward to Sunday." She put down the phone and spoke out loud, "He does seem a bit uncertain, but nothing ventured, nothing gained." She knew she should try to treat it as an adventure.

Valerie surveyed the shoe rack at the bottom of her wardrobe. What to wear for a visit to a vineyard? Her favourite shoes were red , with two inch heels. They wouldn't do. Then there were the black court shoes she wore for work. It was only May so she couldn't go in bare feet and sandals but she always felt unfeminine in boots. She supposed she could brighten them up with a floral blouse and black trousers. It wasn't the usual outfit for a first date but then, this wasn't like a normal date, was it ? She knew she would be comfortable and relaxed. They were long, elegant boots, not sturdy walking boots, she didn't own any of those, but they would have to do. She hoped it wouldn't be muddy.

The sky was overcast when the taxi drew up at the entrance to the vineyard. Valerie hoped she'd been invited to lunch. It hadn't really been very clear.

When Cyril came to the gate to greet her she realised his photograph had not done him justice. His bright blue eyes matched the check shirt he was wearing and his hands, when he shook hers, were slim but strong.

She felt a shiver of anticipation which surprised her.

"Oh, you've got sensible footwear," he declared. "How thoughtful. Would you like a coffee before we do the tour?"

"That would be nice. What time shall I ask the taxi to return?"

"Oh, I don't know. I hadn't thought," Cyril stuttered and she was reminded of her initial fears.

"It's best to miss the school times," the taxi driver said. "Shall we say 4.30 unless you ring and say otherwise?"

"Or 2.30?" she queried, looking at Cyril for confirmation.

"4.30 is perfect," he said, "Time for a leisurely

lunch."

Valerie relaxed. Perhaps it wasn't going to be such a bad day after all.

True to his word Cyril took her round the vineyard, not that there was much to see, although he described the different kinds of grapes and explained why they did so well.

"It's a combination of the soil and the location. A south east facing slope, sheltered from the north winds by those trees."

"I thought the prevailing winds were from the west," Valerie said, trying to sound knowledgeable.

"Most of the time, west or south west. Would you like to try some of the wine? We have sparkling white or rose´.

"I'd like the white, please," and I'd like a sit down, Valerie thought and was relieved to find the lunch was a plate of cheese ploughman's.

After two large glasses of wine Valerie found it hard to concentrate on Cyril's conversation. He seemed to have only one interest, the vineyard, and was only too happy to explain the business side of the operation as well as the growing side. In fact it was four o'clock before he asked her about herself and by then she was ready to go home. She consoled herself with the thought that she still had the visit to the cinema with Richard to look forward to.

On Saturday afternoon Richard greeted her warmly and gave her a peck on the cheek when they met in the foyer of the cinema. "Would you like some chocolates?" he asked, while they waited for the previous audience to emerge.

Valerie blushed. "Not really, but an ice cream in the interval wouldn't be too decadent, would it?"

Following him she couldn't help remarking, "You've got tickets near the back."

"Yes, I can't stand being too near the speakers. Do you mind?"

"Not at all. I don't like being too near the screen, either."

Valerie usually liked musicals but she would have enjoyed it more if Richard had not rested his arm on her shoulder. It seemed too familiar, too soon and, frankly, too teenage! Not only that, it gave her a crick in her neck with tension.

When he drove her home she turned to thank him and he said softly, "We didn't have much time to talk, did we? Have you ever been to the Pavilion in Brighton?"

"No, my husband wasn't into history."

"I'd like to show you round, and perhaps we could visit the aquarium, too. I'd like to see you again."

"I'd like that," said Valerie, and meant it. That was what she had been looking for, wasn't it-someone to take her out and about?

"He's quite charming," she thought later, "but there's no spark. I just don't want to hurt his feelings."

She was still trying to think of a way to let Richard down gently when she arrived at the allotment on Sunday afternoon. This was her favourite place and she had been neglecting it.

Laurence and Joe were hard at work digging out last year's vegetables and clearing a patch for new seeds.

"He's never happy until it's been raked to a fine tilth," Joe called out. "It's good to see you back, Valerie. I've shifted a few weeds for you, nothing strenuous."

"Thanks, Joe. I thought it was about time I took a look. Nothing stands still for ever, does it?"

"Let us know if you need a hand."

"Thank you, Joe. I'll just potter for a bit. So many memories."

She thought back to the weeks after the funeral when Joe and Laurence had come over to where she was hunched over some sad looking sprouts.

"We thought you might like to take this home with you," Joe had said as Laurence held out a large pot containing a plant with thick, shiny green leaves. "Something for the home."

Valerie had felt tears come to her eyes. "A rubber plant! That's very thoughtful," she'd muttered. "Thank you, both. I think I've got just the place for it. I'll call it Bertie."

"We'll drive round with it," Laurence had offered. "It's too heavy for you to carry."

They must have bought it at the garden centre, thought Valerie. It's ages since I went there and it was always our place for anniversaries and birthdays. She was beginning to feel maudlin again. The pain of her loss was only just beginning to fade and places she had been to with James always brought her up short with the awareness that someone was missing.

Was now the time to look for another man in her life? She was only 38. She couldn't imagine being alone for ever. As usual she was torn between carrying on as usual and trying something new.

But now it was time to show her friends that she could tend an allotment perfectly well by herself. The exercise would do her good. She didn't need to go to the gym while she had her plot to care for.

Chapter 3

The Brighton Pavilion turned out to be fascinating and Richard was amusing company.

"I've prepared lunch for us at my flat," he declared, to her surprise. "It's not far."

She didn't know what to say. She was getting into a situation where she would find things awkward at least. Yet she couldn't admit that she didn't want to go with him, not after all the attention he had given her. She needed time to work out how to react. If only there was someone she could ask. She'd begun to give Bertie a personality. What did she think he would say? 'Be tough, woman. If you don't like what is happening be honest and say so.'

But Richard was big and strong, and she didn't know how he would react if she annoyed him. Still, he was a policeman. He wouldn't do anything to break the law, would he?

She tried to stay calm as he ushered her into a smartly furnished room with a table at one end and a suite, TV and music centre at the other.

"Make yourself at home," he told her. "I'll just get everything from the kitchen."

"Can I see?" Valerie asked.

"The kitchen? Of course. I'll show you the rest later. Come in."

The kitchen was long and thin with a coffee and cream décor and a tiled floor. All the appliances looked brand new and there were plenty of cupboards with shiny gold handles.

"It's beautiful," Valerie gasped.

"It's functional." He opened the fridge and added items to the tray on the worktop.

"If you'll take these two glasses I'll bring the rest. I hope you like salmon."

It was a much more elegant feast that she could have supplied but Valerie could hardly swallow as she wondered what would happen next. I'm being silly, she told herself. He said we would visit the aquarium this afternoon.

Richard brought her coffee, added liqueur and asked what music she liked. She almost said Frank Sinatra but thought that might be too romantic so she said traditional jazz. He looked surprised. "The nearest thing I've got to that is Big Band stuff. How about Ella Fitzgerald?"

As Ella's sultry tones filled the room he came and sat down next to her. I shouldn't have picked the settee, Valerie thought, but it was too late.

"What have you been getting up to, since I saw you last?" Richard enquired.

"Not much. I did see the other gentleman Fiona found for me."

"Someone else? You were two timing me?"

"I thought we were all given choices. Didn't you have two?"

"No, I didn't. It never occurred to me that we were given options at the same time." He sounded angry. "It was made out that they spent time and effort finding a perfect match. I read all about you and I was so sure that you were right for me. Then we met and I liked you straight away. I thought we were getting close. I didn't realise you were just playing the field."

He jumped to his feet, his face red and his fists clenched. "This is nothing like what I expected." He looked quite intimidating and Valerie wasn't sure what he would do next.

"I suppose you want me to leave," she stuttered, almost choking as she got the words out.

He looked as if he was struggling for control.

"I'm sorry," he gasped at last. "It's so difficult, isn't it? I was hoping..." He sat down heavily in a chair.

Valerie didn't know what to do. He looked vulnerable, hunched in his seat and she realised he had been putting on an act. He was actually as nervous as she was.

"I understand. Shall we go to the aquarium or would you like me to leave you in peace?"

"I need to do something. I don't suppose you'd like to see our gym?"

"These flats have their own gym?"

"Yes, and a swimming pool. Hang on while I change and I'll show you."

Valerie began to relax. He wasn't going to take her into the bedroom. She was safe and now he had shown his vulnerable side she began to like him more.

They were the only two people in the gym and for a while she watched Richard as he ran on the treadmill and then moved to the rowing machine.

He was quite muscular and she couldn't help admiring his physique but when he indicated that he was going to have a quick shower she retreated to the lobby, telling herself not to get carried away. She needed to know more about him before she could make a judgement and much more before she could allow herself to get emotionally involved.

I mustn't compare him to James, she told herself, but it was difficult. They had been together for nine years and their lives had developed a rhythm, a pattern, that she felt contented with.

She wondered, now, if they would have gone on like that for ever. It wasn't that they didn't have plans and ambitions. James wanted to move out into the country. He was investigating solar panels but their house was unsuitable.

It must come from being the younger sibling, she thought. I'm used to being a follower.

But circumstances had changed and now she was in charge of her own destiny. It was a daunting thought and she was determined not to make a mistake.

"Next time you come, bring a swimming costume," Richard said cheerfully when he came out of the shower looking refreshed. "If there is a next time."

"It would be good for me," Valerie replied. "Thank you."

"I'm sorry I was rushing things and, be warned, I like you a lot but I'm the jealous type, Valerie."

"There's no need to be. I won't be seeing the other man again." Valerie replied, but she was still concerned. She needed to get home and think over everything that had happened. It had all been too much, too soon. What was she going to tell Fiona?

"I don't know whether to see him again or not," she found herself speaking out loud to Bertie when she returned to her own kitchen.

"If only Fiona had found Richard someone else, so that he could know what it was like to have to choose." She sighed. "That really was an adventure. I wouldn't want to go through that again." Bertie, of course, was silent.

On her next visit to the allotment there was a thumping and grunting coming from the plot next to hers.

"Joe," Valerie called out. "You're putting in a lot of

effort with that digging. What's the matter?"

Joe paused. "You guessed. I've had some bad news."

"Medical?"

"No, it's Laurence. He's moving away."

"Laurence. Why? I thought he was planning what to grow this season."

"So did I. He's going to live in France. He's had a promotion. He couldn't turn it down."

"You won't give up the allotment?"

"Oh, no. No fear of that. It's the only thing that keeps me sane and I love all the fresh vegetables."

"I don't know what I'd do without your delicious tomatoes. Can't you find someone else to share?"

"Well, there is someone I could ask." He smiled at her and nodded his head.

"What, me? How could I do that?"

"Why don't we pop into the shed for a cuppa and discuss it. I have chocolate biscuits."

So Valerie found herself with a mug of tea, listening to Joe explain how, if she had one end of his plot for salads he would put a row of currant bushes across the middle and use the rest for vegetables. "We'd still have spinach and potatoes and sweet corn. I'll not bother with the beans and there's room next to the shed for the tomatoes. You must admit we're both struggling on our own."

"In more ways than one," Valerie added and went on to tell him about Ocean Introductions.

She made it sound so amusing he laughed out loud.

"I'm seeing one of them again," said Valerie, "but I'm not sure. I can't quite figure out what is wrong."

"It takes time to get to know someone properly," Joe said. "I should know. After all I've given him.

19

Laurence has even taken our prize orchid with him."

Valerie went home that evening determined to make an effort with Richard.

"My three month special offer is almost over," she mused. "If I want to stay on Fiona's books I'll have to pay for another six months."

She seemed to hear Bertie's voice saying, "Wait until after your next date and see how you feel then."

When she saw Fiona she explained that the meeting with Cyril had been a disaster and she needed advice on how to proceed. She said Richard was becoming a friend and that was enough for the moment. Perhaps she would come back at a later date.

"If Richard wants to see someone else that's OK. He might find someone he likes more than me."

"That's not the attitude," Fiona responded. "I've a feeling it will turn out well for both of you."

But Valerie had decided it was too exhausting to keep meeting new men and next time Richard called she told him she was taking a week's holiday. She'd considered singles coach tours but, in the end, decided she would just take a train to somewhere she had never been and book into a hotel. To make it worthwhile it had to be somewhere special, somewhere she had always wanted to go. She didn't fancy going abroad but there was somewhere she and James had talked about, the Scilly Isles. She had heard that it was like going back in time and that the island of Tresco had a wonderful garden that stayed fascinating all year round. She had a choice. Should she take the train to Cornwall and go across on the ferry or fly from Southampton? Not wanting to face a rough crossing she decided on the latter. She would go for five days, that was long enough to be away from home. She could forget all her plans and obligations and just relax and explore.

She chose a B and B on the main island, St Mary's, and spent the Saturday morning making suitable purchases, sensible walking shoes, a strong haversack, a new thermos flask and a pair of binoculars. She wasn't a bird watcher but there was something about the idea of islands that made her imagine herself scanning the horizon. She already had a good camera and, of course, her mobile phone took pictures, although she rarely used it. There hadn't been anyone to call for some time, had there? She didn't want to contact anybody from Ocean Introductions. She wanted to try to enjoy her own company and perhaps converse with fellow travellers without the tension that seeking romance incurred.

Chapter 4

In fact, flying to the islands felt liberating and when they arrived in warm sunshine and she found her clean, bright B and B she felt sure she had made the right decision. She could hardly wait to get unpacked and take a walk to the harbour. Her room was as expected, with delicately patterned wallpaper and a double bed covered in a floral quilt. The information folder on the bedside table gave her the house timetable, including optional packed lunches and a variety of different breakfasts which included eggs benedict, something she had never tasted. She would have to find a restaurant for dinner, which was slightly daunting, but meanwhile she would get out and explore before it got dark.

James had always headed for the Information Centre when they were away and she did the same. She wanted to make sure she could book a trip to Tresco and felt sure they could suggest somewhere for an evening meal. She would buy a postcard for the girls in the office and Richard, if she could remember his address. She knew the block of flats but had no idea of the postcode. Perhaps she wouldn't bother. He might feel hurt that he hadn't been asked to accompany her. She had the feeling he could become possessive.

Standing by the harbour wall, looking out over the sea, she took in a deep breath and felt a wide grin spreading over her face. She could be happy again, she told herself. There was a big, wide world out there with places and people to discover. This was the start of a new chapter in her life and she was in the perfect place to experience it.

The assistant in the Information Centre gave her a number of restaurants to try, including a fish restaurant that had outside tables which appealed to Valerie. She felt uncertain about eating alone in public and felt that would look less intimate. She didn't want to look as if she was waiting for someone who hadn't turned up. She was content to eat early. The fresh air was making her hungry and she was not inclined to dress up. She returned to the B and B for a jacket, changed her shoes and then strolled slowly to the restaurant.

She ordered cod and chips, which came with a choice of peas and tried a half of a local beer. It was a good meal but nobody approached her and she began to feel isolated so she went without a dessert and, paying with cash, walked back down to the harbour. There was music coming from one of the public houses on the front and she willed herself to venture inside.

Everyone looked like regulars but the barman gave her a warm smile so she asked for a cider and found a seat in the corner.

"You like sea shanties?" the man at the next table asked her.

"I've not heard many," Valerie replied, "But they sound very jolly and the harmonies are great."

"Can I buy you a drink?" he said, moving across to sit with her.

"No thank you. I've only just got one," she said, stiffly.

"You on holiday, then?"

"Yes."

"On your own?" His breath was in her face and she was afraid he was a little drunk.

"No, I'm with my sister," she lied. "She's on leave

23

from the army. I'm meeting her later."

"Is she as pretty as you? Perhaps we could make up a foursome?" He nodded towards a large bearded man wearing a thick sweater who was standing by the bar.

"I don't think so. She isn't interested in men." Valerie's heart was thumping. She felt cornered.

"Pity. We don't get many attractive young women in here. The place seems to cater for the older generation. Would you like to go somewhere more lively?"

His hand was on her knee and she was feeling very uncomfortable. "That's good of you to invite me," she said through gritted teeth, "but it's time I met her."

"I'll come with you," he said, standing up and grabbing hold of her arm but she was too quick for him. As the music started up again she shook him off, slid out of her seat and headed for the door. Once outside she took a quick left and then ran down some steps to a narrow lane that wound round the headland away from the town. When she thought she had gone far enough she decided to head for the sea and find her way back along the front. Being on her own was not as easy as she had imagined.

She sat down heavily on a bench by the harbour wall. She was shaking. Could one be hot and cold at the same time? Her body felt as if it was burning but the sweat on her arms was chilling and her eyes were watering.

She'd escaped, but would she see the man again? Come on, Valerie, she told herself, People have suffered much worse. You can look after yourself, can't you? She was hugging herself to try to curb the shivering and gradually began to feel calmer. She wasn't hurt. When she was younger she would have shrugged it off as experience. She wished she'd been brave enough to hit him. The thought made her smile-just imagine, causing a scene in a public house! She really would have to toughen up. She'd been too careless. It wasn't as if she hadn't been warned.

Still, she had the trip to Tresco to look forward to and there would be a crowd of visitors on the boat – no danger then of getting accosted.

The gardens at Tresco were divided into glades, like rooms, with the trees and plants discretely labelled. There were palms from tropical countries and arbours with statues and mosaic decorations. There were more steps than she had anticipated but it made for exciting views and Valerie was enchanted by the place.

Eventually she sat down on a stone bench and closed her eyes, drinking in the scent of the flowers and listening to the wind in the trees.

She couldn't help thinking how James would have loved these gardens, but with a different feeling from that she was experiencing. His was an eagerness to copy, to make his own version, while she was happy just to wallow in the atmosphere and hope to retain the memory. I must take some photographs, she thought, and reached for her phone.

"Would you like me to take a photograph of you, by the trellis?" asked a polite voice from behind her.

Valerie looked up. The voice belonged to a white haired man in a grey gilet over a striped shirt and green corduroy trousers. He was wearing hiking boots and carrying a rucksack, with a pair of binoculars round his neck.

"Well, thank you," Valerie replied. "I haven't taken any photos yet – but I would like to be in at least one of them."

The man smiled and held out his hand. "David Constantine. I'm happy to help."

"I'm Valerie Davies." She blushed as she handed him her phone and turned to look where he had directed her.

"That's right. I have the sun behind me," David encouraged as she posed by a low brick wall.

He seemed to know exactly how to use her phone and , for a second, she wondered if she could trust him not to run away with it. Then she relaxed as he came towards her to return it.

"Look, will these do? I took three."

"I do look a bit nervous, don't I?" Valerie said, "But that one is better."

"You have a lovely smile."

"Thank you." She accepted the compliment with good grace, expecting him to move on, but he didn't.

"Are you on holiday, here?" he asked.

"Yes, at St Mary's."

"So am I. So you are going back on the later boat?"

"Yes."

"Is anyone meeting you on the other side?"

Alarm bells began to ring in Valerie's head. "I'm not sure," she lied.

"I only asked because I am dining alone and would be grateful if you would join me. I'm sorry. It was presumptuous of me. It's just that I'm not used to being on my own."

"You've had a recent loss?"

"Yes, my wife. We've been here before, lots of times. It was her favourite place. I should never have come back without her."

"It's making you sad."

"Yes, but my daughter says I must look forward,

26

not back. It isn't easy after forty years. But I mustn't spoil your holiday. Thank you for listening to me."

"Thank you for taking the photos. Would you like me to take one of you?"

"Oh, no. That would make me even more miserable. I have so many of us here together. I'm taking up too much of your time," and he scuttled away into the trees as if he couldn't leave her fast enough.

I was a bit unkind,Valerie thought. I could have accepted his invitation. Perhaps if I see him on the boat I might consider it.

It was while she was waiting to board the boat for St Mary's that she saw David again. He looked a little more cheerful, Valerie thought, and smiled at him. "Hallo, David."

"Valerie! Did you enjoy the trip?"

"Very much. Are those binoculars for birds or views?"

"Both. I dabble in painting. Now I have to go back to my hotel and try to capture some of the things I have seen today. I would ask if you'd like to see some but that's such a cliché. I expect you have plans..."

"Actually, David, I don't have plans for this evening. If your invitation still stands I would love to join you for dinner, on one condition, you let me pay for myself."

"How very modern, I've a better idea – let me treat you tonight and you can buy me lunch tomorrow, or tea, if you have time."

"Are you eating at your hotel?"

"Yes. I'll show you. The food is very good. You will make an old man very happy."

Valerie giggled. She supposed he was at least twenty years older than her but she hadn't come away to find a new partner, had she? She didn't enjoy eating alone. She didn't like to admit it but the holiday was making her feel a little lonely.

Chapter 5

It was fun, choosing something to wear for dinner. The hotel had looked very expensive and she'd only brought one dress with her. It was green, with short sleeves and a wrap around skirt. She had a colourful necklace that she liked to wear with it. She hadn't brought any of her more precious jewellery.

Once seated, with a steaming plate of carbonara in front of her and a glass of white wine she began to enjoy the evening.

David was an attentive listener and she found herself telling him how, after her husband had died, her friends kept telling her to get a pet, a dog or a cat, but she didn't want to be tied to the house. She hadn't wanted a bird in a cage and she certainly didn't want a little animal to look after – she'd never liked hamsters or gerbils.

"I told them I could manage but they caught me talking to myself so I had to pretend I would consider their suggestion."

"And you never felt like trying again?" David asked.

"Perhaps," she replied, not ready to tell him about Ocean Introductions, "but I'm getting used to being by myself."

"Hence the holiday."

"Yes, and that's enough about me. You were going to show me some of your sketches."

"Not etchings!" David laughed, "I'll go up and fetch some after our meal. Now, what can I tempt you with?"

His eyes twinkled and Valerie suddenly felt she was about to enjoy the evening.

It wasn't until she checked her watch that Valerie realised it was ten o'clock and she hadn't warned her landlady she might be late. The meal had been as good as her companion had promised and his stories about his life and passions had kept her enthralled. When she saw his sketches she recognised a true talent and when he offered one to her as a gift she did not refuse.

"I like the one of the seagull on the harbour wall," Valerie said, "but not if it is too much."

"Not at all. This evening has given me more pleasure than I could express. You're delightful company, my dear."

Valerie couldn't imagine that her conversation had been that exceptional, although she had relaxed enough to tell him some of her adventures with Ocean Introductions, doing her best to make them entertaining. Perhaps being in the presence of a complete stranger made them sound less nerve racking than they had been.

"Are you going swimming with Richard?" David asked.

"I think I might. There's more to him than I have allowed myself to discover."

"I think you're very brave."

"Brave or desperate."

"I don't call it desperate to want someone to share ones life with – especially since you had a happy marriage."

"You've been very cunning, getting me to tell you so much about myself. I don't know much about you except that you can do these beautiful paintings."

"I express myself in my work. I'm not very good with words."

"I don't believe that, David, but you didn't tell me

what job you had."

"No longer. I used to be a teacher. I took Art and Physical Education. I don't look like it now but I used to be fit and healthy. I cycled everywhere. It was a good life, with hours that suited me."

"And long holidays?"

"Yes, it gave us the chance to travel."

"And your wife, what did she do?"

"She was what they call a stay-at-home mum, even when the children went to school."

"And do they live near you, the children?"

"Paula does – she's a good girl. She's a care worker so she knows how to look after an old codger like me. Greg is abroad, with the navy. I don't hear from him much."

"I envy you. I didn't think I was bothered about having children until I lost James and then I realised how it would have been a comfort to know that part of him continued into the future."

"You still have time. You'll find someone, probably when you're not looking."

She blushed at his kind words. "I hope so, but I must go now. I don't know when the landlady locks the door."

"It's usually midnight at these places but I'll see you home."

"Thank you, David. It's been a lovely evening."

"How long are you here? Remember, you owe me lunch."

"I'll call you. It might have to be a picnic."

"What an excellent idea. I'll look forward to it."

And so will I, thought Valerie.

Valerie's landlady was kind enough to make a picnic for two. There were sausage rolls, sandwiches, two pots of yogurt, biscuits and cheese and two blueberry muffins. When she asked Valerie if she wanted a flask Valerie was stumped. "I don't know. How about two little cartons of apple juice? I think we might end up in a pub."

"You'll need something warm if it gets cold," came the response, "but perhaps your friend has another idea, maybe a bottle of wine?"

"It's not that kind of picnic," Valerie replied. "He's old enough to be my father."

"They're the ones you have to watch."

"Maybe." For a second Valerie considered telling her about the previous day but she stopped herself. It made her feel foolish to think about it. She would put it out of her mind and enjoy the day with David.

It turned out to be a very pleasant excursion. They walked along empty lanes and across cliff tops, where Valerie could use her binoculars to spot sea birds. David paused by an old church and made a sketch and they had their picnic in the shelter of a small copse.

By late afternoon Valerie was beginning to flag and was grateful when they stopped at a wayside inn.

"I think there's a bus once an hour," David said. "I'll just check."

When he came back he had a concerned look on his face. "They stop at five o'clock. We'll have to get a taxi."

"Then let's have supper here," Valerie suggested, looking at the blackboard on the wall.

"Macaroni cheese," David mused.

"With garlic bread," Valerie added. "Sounds good to me."

And it was.

By nine o'clock Valerie was back in Honeysuckle cottage, full of fresh air and good food. She had told David she was spending her final day shopping for presents. She didn't want him to think that he had to entertain her for the whole holiday. She had considered swimming in the sea but he'd warned her that the water was very cold so she took a book down to the harbour to read. She had vegetable soup and a crusty roll in a harbour cafe and went back to the B and B to pack.

David was staying for an extra day but she had the address and telephone number of his home near Oxford and she had promised to let him know what happened next with her introductions.

"I'll write, and send some photographs of where I live," she told him.

She didn't expect to see him before she left but there was a ring on the doorbell early in the morning.

"I'd like you to have this," David said, standing on the doorstep. "I hope you've got room for it, and I'm not too late."

"What is it?"

"Just a little painting of Tresco. It isn't framed, of course, but I'd like you to have it."

"Thank you, David, but I didn't..."

"Your company was all I could wish for," he smiled. "Bon Voyage," and he hurried away.

Chapter 6

The taxi dropped Valerie off at her front gate and she walked slowly along the path, recognising that the roses needed dead heading. Then she paused. Something wasn't right. She felt a shiver of foreboding. What was different? The curtains. She was sure she had left the curtains of the living room open, but now they were closed. Someone had been in the house while she was away!

Her heart began to thump as she inserted the key in the lock. Were they still there? Had they done any damage? Was anything stolen?

As soon as she opened the door she could feel a draught. She dropped her case and ran into the kitchen. Sure enough, the back door was ajar. Someone had forced the lock and now it wasn't completely closed. She pushed it shut with her foot and stood in front of it, turning to survey the room. To her relief it looked untouched.

She moved into the dining room. At first it, too, looked as she had left it, but then she noticed the sideboard door ajar. Bottles of drink had been taken, along with cutlery from the drawers. A few ornaments were missing, too, but nothing seemed damaged.

It was when she moved to the front room that the theft became obvious. Her television and set box had gone, along with her music centre and some of her CDs. They must have had time to choose the ones they wanted, she thought, fear giving way to anger. I wonder what I'll find upstairs? She didn't dare look until she had phoned the police.

"Try not to touch anything," was the advice, but she hoped that didn't apply to the kitchen. She needed a cup of tea. Her hands were shaking so much she poured boiling water all over the table. Frustrated, she grabbed some sheets of kitchen paper and began frantically mopping up, her actions getting more and more violent as she proceeded.

Sobbing, she threw the sodden paper in the bin and sat down heavily.

"Oh, Bertie," she cried, looking at her precious plant. "Now what am I going to do?"

The milk in the fridge was still usable and she added two spoonfuls of sugar to her cup. She didn't want to sit in the rooms that had been so obviously desecrated so she sat in the kitchen and waited for the police.

"You look so good, standing there," she said to Bertie. "Thank goodness they didn't knock you over or steal you. I don't suppose they even noticed you. It's something to be thankful for."

It was a long wait and by the time she heard the doorbell she was eager to go to the toilet. Flustered, she opened the door to two uniformed officers, one male, one female. Hurriedly she explained what she had seen and then, apologising, rushed upstairs. The toilet was separate from the bathroom and when she had relieved herself she went to wash her hands. Here, again, someone had been there before her. The bathroom cabinet had been ransacked and pills and jars discarded, some even left in the bath.

She gave a wry smile. Nothing stronger than paracetamol there, Valerie thought, trying to pull herself together.

The policeman called up the stairs, "Have you searched up there?"

"No, not yet. Come up."

She watched the policewoman push at the

bedroom door with her gloved hand, not touching the handle. Valerie's heart was thumping again. Why couldn't she stop shaking? What would they find?

All the drawers and cupboards had been opened. Her clothes were strewn across the bed, her jewellery box emptied and treasured photos and letters scattered over the floor.

Valerie burst into tears again. "Why?" she sobbed. "Why do they have to destroy everything?"

"We need to get someone up here," the policewoman said. "Can you sleep elsewhere, tonight?"

"You mean, in the other room?"

"No, another house."

"I don't think I want to. Can we look in the other rooms?"

"What do you use the front box room for?"

"Oh, gosh. That's the office. My computer is in there." She followed the policewoman to the doorway, trying to stifle her sobs and control her racing heartbeats.

"That's a surprise," commented the policewoman, "It's still there."

Valerie dried her eyes. "It's ten years old. I don't think anyone would want it. It was probably too heavy. The only other room is the back bedroom. I don't use it. It's for guests."

The policewoman followed her along the landing. Valerie gave a sigh of relief. The room looked untouched.

"I do keep a few bits and pieces of clothing in here," Valerie said, hopefully, opening the wardrobe doors. Nothing appeared to have been disturbed.

"We would rather you slept elsewhere," said the policewoman, "Unless you have someone who could

36

stay here with you?"

"I've just been away for a week," Valerie snapped. "I need to get sorted before work on Monday. If I promise to stick to the bathroom, the kitchen and this room can I stay here?"

"Well, thieves don't usually return. I'll check with SOCO. My colleague should be finished in the kitchen by now."

"There's no one I would want to see this," Valerie muttered, the reality of her situation dawning on her at last. Straightening her shoulders in an effort to convince herself as much as the police she said "I'm OK. I have friends I can call on if I need to. First, I need a bath."

They returned to the ground floor.

"They came through the back gate," the policeman told them. "It's only got a bolt, hasn't it? I'll take some photographs. Have you got any of the items they have stolen? Are you insured?"

"I never thought of that," Valerie said. "All the papers are upstairs in the office."

"It's best you tell them quickly. Make a list of everything that's missing. If you have photos we need to see them. Did you have money in the house, bank books etc.?"

"I had my cheque book and credit cards with me but there were bank statements in the bureau."

"Warn your bank today. We'll need to talk to your neighbours to see if they heard anything. You live alone?"

"Yes, and I want to stay here tonight."

"We can't leave anyone with you but I've secured the back door. There was a bolt you hadn't used and I have pushed a barrow up to the back gate. If you don't need to go out in the garden I suppose you could stay."

The garden, thought Valerie. I haven't checked to see if anything is damaged. Well, it's too late now. "I'll ring work and tell them I might not be in on Monday."

"Good thinking. That's probably the soonest we can finish up here. Here's the number for Victim Support. The more you can tell us about what's missing, the better. We'll wait to hear from you."

At least they left the washing machine, Valerie said to herself. I can unpack some of my holiday clothes. What to do next? She'd promised not to use the front room so she left the curtains closed. She was desperate for advice and considered texting Richard.

She turned on the water heater and went to look for her insurance details. She was suddenly very tired. Maybe calling Richard was not a good idea. It was impossible to think. She wanted it all to go away. She had a tin of soup in the larder and some frozen bread in the freezer. She would have to shop for food the next day but now she was drained, so exhausted that all she wanted to do was flop into bed and sleep.

She'd make a quick supper and have her bath. Doing anything else would be just too much.

She was just taking the washing out of the machine when the doorbell rang. It was her next door neighbour.

"Sorry to bother you, Valerie," she said, "but the police have just told me what happened. Are you OK?"

"Yes, Judy, just tired."

"Is there anything we can do? We didn't see anything. I'm so sorry. Who would do this? Who knew you were going away?"

"It wasn't a secret, you knew, the postman knew, Joe at the allotment knew and the people at Ocean Introductions, oh, and Richard, my policeman friend."

"Have you told him?"

"Not yet. I feel such a fool. Judy, the place doesn't seem the same, somehow. I used to love it but now just looking at it makes me want to cry. At least they left my plants behind," and she shuddered.

"Come round to our place and have a cup of tea. You might feel more like coping with it then."

"Thanks, but I don't want to leave at the moment. I feel as though if I did I'd never want to come back. I'm not really thinking straight at present. I mean to shop in the morning but if I don't I'll give you a list, OK?"

"You're staying here?"

"Yes, in the spare room."

"You're very brave."

"Not really. They won't come back. There's nothing left to steal."

"Nor at our place. I wish we could be more help."

"If Peter could point his hose over my back garden I'd be grateful," Valerie said. "I'm not supposed to use the back door until the police have been back."

"You'll be waiting for ever. You know how short staffed they are."

"They said Monday."

"Well give me that list in the morning. Are you OK for milk?"

"It might last. They didn't take the fridge."

"Just knock if you need anything. I'll leave you in peace. Goodnight, Valerie."

"Goodnight, Judy, and thank you."

Chapter 7

It was strange not having a television. Valerie began to realise how much she relied on it for entertainment. The burglars had left the radio she kept in the cupboard and she tried to make conversation with Bertie but to no avail. Somehow the same questions kept racing round her head and she couldn't think of any answers.

It was irrational, she knew, but she wanted to throw away everything the burglars might have touched. Instead she washed the lightest clothing and put the more bulky items aside to take to the cleaners.

She needed to keep busy to stop herself focussing on the burglary so decided to spend Saturday baking and, when it turned out to be sunny, clipping the hedge in the tiny front garden.

All the houses in the terrace had flint and brick front walls but a few had added privet hedges for screening and as James had kept his bike in the front it had been ideal. She had always worried that he might have an accident on his bike, in spite of knowing he was a skilled and careful rider and it was a bitter irony that he had perished in the sea, not on a road. She had given the machine to his friends to sell. She couldn't bear to see it outside the house every time she went through the front door.

By Sunday, tired of her own company and with fresh food bought for her the day before, she packed a bag and headed for the allotment. But the sky clouded over while she was busy with the hoe and she stood in the shelter of Joe's shed watching the rain pour down and feeling nothing was ever going to go right. Finishing her flask of coffee and, with no-one else on the site she decided the only place to dry off was the nearby pub.

Unfortunately, it being Sunday lunchtime, the place was quite full and she looked in vain for an empty table.

"Mrs Davies?" enquired a voice at her shoulder. Standing beside her was a familiar figure. Where had she seen him before?

"Hallo," Valerie replied, trying desperately to remember his name. "Is this your local?"

"Yes, it's Lucy's birthday so we brought her here for lunch." He turned and waved at a sad looking woman and a teenager. "Why don't you come and join us, if you're on your own?"

"Oh, I couldn't intrude on a family party."

"Please." He had a nervous air about him and his wife had a concerned look on her face. What's going on here? Valerie wondered.

Reluctantly she followed the man to the table and sat down next to his daughter.

"We'll have the roast, shall we?" he said cheerfully.

"You know Lucy doesn't like any meat except chicken," snapped his wife.

"Yes, dear. Barbara, this is Mrs Davies, Valerie, I believe? You want yorkshires, Lucy?"

Valerie nodded at Barbara and smiled at Lucy, who was wriggling in her seat. She looked about fourteen years old. This didn't seem like her idea of a birthday celebration.

"What can I order for you, Valerie?" asked Eric.

"I'd like the chicken too, please," Valerie replied.

He rose and went to the bar and Lucy took the opportunity to whisper, "They've had a row."

"Oh, I'm sorry to hear that."

"It's about work. Mum's been offered more hours.

41

He's being difficult about it."

"It's a shame, on your birthday."

"Doesn't matter. I'm going out tonight."

"I hope they resolve the matter."

"Mum will win. She always does," and she turned to face the table as Eric returned to join his wife.

"We heard about the burglary," Barbara said. "Was much taken?"

"The TV and some jewellery. I was on holiday."

"It's such a quiet street," Eric said and Valerie realised where she had seen him before. He was the relief postman. The one who delivered her letters when the regular one was away.

"I doubt if they'll come back to me but I'm changing the locks on the back gate. The house doesn't feel the same."

"You won't move?" Barbara asked.

"No, but I might redecorate, make it feel different."

The arrival of their meals halted conversation and Valerie was happy to see they all seemed to relax. Perhaps having someone else with them put their problems into perspective. She hoped so.

She couldn't bear to go back to her empty home straight after lunch so she went to the garden centre instead and found herself looking at the outside furniture. After all, it was summer. If she sat in the garden she wouldn't see the empty spaces in the lounge. She took some brochures home with her to help her choose, and she'd think about a new carpet. It was time to start renewing things.

Monday morning Valerie was washing up her breakfast things when the doorbell rang. The investigators had arrived. One concentrated on the back door and the other dusted door handles and checked out the lounge and then went upstairs.

"We have to take your prints, I'm afraid," he said. "to eliminate you. Can you come down to the station?"

"Of course. I've a free day. Can I use the whole house when you've finished?"

"Yes. You need to get the place secure as quickly as possible."

"Can I get you a tea or coffee?"

"No, thanks. We've more to see. We'll let you know if there are any developments."

That was quick, Valerie thought, as she watched them drive away. Now what do I do? I suppose I had better go to the police station. I'll see Judy first. Her husband is a builder. He'll know someone who can fix my back door.

Judy promised to get Pete to look in that evening and Valerie got the bus into town. After having her fingerprints taken she decided to choose a new TV. The choice was bewildering.

"I've got an aerial," she told the assistant, "but no set box. I'll have to start all over again."

"Who were you with? Was it free or did you have Sky?"

"It was free, but it needed updating. I don't want an enormous screen."

After some discussion she made her selection and agreed delivery the following Saturday.

The cafe´ on the pier was her next stop, for coffee and a muffin. She decided to pop into Ocean Introductions and tell them what had happened.

"Hallo, Valerie," Fiona greeted her warmly. "Just the person I wanted to see. I know you weren't sure about carrying on but I think I've found someone to suit you."

Valerie didn't have time to tell her about the burglary as the file was in her hand. The man's photograph was promising.

"He's a journalist," Fiona told her. "He's worked all over the world, probably been too busy to settle down -now wants to before it's too late."

"But he's only 32," Valerie exclaimed.

"Does that matter?"

"That he's younger than me? I suppose not. I'll probably bore him to death."

"Give it a try. There must be something in your profile that attracted him. As you don't drive I suggested the Pavilion. He knew it. He said, "Ah – Pier of the Year.""

Well it's nice and public, thought Valerie. "OK, but I'm back at work. It will have to be Saturday. It could be busy."

"Read his resume´. He sounds very interesting."

"I'm not getting my hopes up," Valerie replied, but something about the smiling face in front of her made her heart flip. "I've never been out with a redhead before. This could be fun."

Chapter 8

"Hi, I'm Connor. You must be Valerie. Can I call you Val?"

The man bounced up to her holding out his hand. Valerie had been sitting in the cafe´ with a cup of coffee for fifteen minutes and was beginning to think of going home when a tall, lanky individual with ginger hair strode through the double doors and looked eagerly round the room.

He's wearing shorts! thought Valerie. Who goes on a date wearing shorts? But his smile was wide and his hand, when it clasped hers, strong and warm.

"I see you have a drink. I'll just get one – anything else I can tempt you with?" he asked.

"No, thanks," Valerie replied, wondering what she had let herself in for. He didn't seem her type at all.

"Funny place, this," Connor remarked. "They used to do jazz but they don't any more."

"People come here because they like to see the sea," Valerie said.

"OK, in the daytime, but at night it's just for the theatre goers I suppose. Do you go to the shows?"

"I'm afraid I don't. I've been to the Dome, but not recently."

"Fancy going to a night club?"

"I'm not sure. I'm not too good with loud music and flashing lights."

"They aren't all like that. There's an Open Mic. Night at the one I go to. I'll take you if you like."

"When?"

"Tonight, pick you up about ten."

Ten o'clock, thought Valerie, just when I'm thinking of going to bed.

"It's not something I've ever done. Where is it?"

"Just over the road. Where's your pad?"

"A bus ride away, but they stop at five. I'll have to get a taxi."

"No need. I've got a car. Give me your address and I'll pick you up."

Valerie couldn't think of a way to avoid telling him. After all, what was there left in the house to steal- and she would soon have all the new security in place. She watched while he put all the details she dictated into his phone.

"Now, tell me your favourite colour," Connor asked.

"Green," Valerie replied without hesitation.

"Ah, yes. You like gardening. I don't have a garden, but I live by the woods. I like brown. Most people don't pick brown, but there's so many different shades-and it's another natural colour , isn't it? Now ask me a question."

The date was beginning to feel like a game and Valerie was starting to enjoy herself.

"Your favourite animal and why," she said.

"A bird – let's think – an eagle, probably a sea eagle, but any of them. They are proud and fierce and look magnificent but they can be trained. I think we'd all like to be able to fly. Yours?"

"Mine is an elephant. They are big and majestic but very caring. They seem to have feelings. If one dies they mourn them."

"Would you always have chosen them?"

"Oh, no," she laughed. "I expect when I was young I would have said a horse, or at least a pony."

"Do you ride?"

"No. I wanted to but my family could never afford it. They weren't the kind that gave their children

46

riding lessons."

"Do you have any brothers or sisters?"

"A sister, but she's in the States."

"And your husband -what was he like, or would you rather not talk about him?"

"James? He was quiet, thoughtful, loved things made out of wood but also liked to keep fit. He enjoyed having an allotment. That's enough about me. Why on earth are you using an Introduction Agency?"

"I've just had bad experiences. I don't seem able to pick the right sort. My last girlfriend was into drugs. The one before that ran off with my best friend and the one before that turned out to be married. I'm always travelling so I don't get time to get to know anyone. I don't have a house. I just rent wherever I go. I was beginning to think I'd left it too late to find someone permanent. Then I tried speed dating. That was a disaster. A friend suggested the Ocean agency so I thought I'd give it a go."

"So you don't live locally?"

"No. I don't live anywhere. I'm always on the move. I'm covering the South Coast at present. Next month I'm off to Australia for six weeks."

"What are you writing about?"

"Changes- how British seaside towns have to change with the times, those big wheels that are going up, British resorts having German Christmas markets, that sort of thing."

"That's really interesting."

"Most of it is commissioned. I don't get to choose what to write about."

"So going to a nightclub in Worthing is really work?"

Connor laughed. "You could say so, but you'll still come?"

"I'm willing to give it a try."

"Good. I'll see you at ten. Would you like a lift now?"

"No, thank you, Connor. I've things to do in town," Valerie replied and was surprised when he gave her a quick peck on the cheek as he left.

What could a fascinating man like him want with someone like her? She would have to try to make herself more trendy for the date. She wished she had someone young and lively to ask. Perhaps Fiona could give her some advice. She wasn't much younger than Valerie but she must know what people wore to night clubs. Valerie had seen young girls in skirts that hardly covered their behinds and tiny crop tops. That wouldn't do for her. Perhaps jeans? She didn't own a pair of jeans but maybe black leggings would do. She did have those, but what to wear with them? If only she had a young friend to shop with.

She had to wait for twenty minutes while Fiona spoke with another client and then she said she could only give Valerie a short time as she was very busy.

"I don't know who else to ask," Valerie began. "Connor has invited me to a night club. I'm not sure what to wear. What would be suitable?"

"It might be dark," Fiona replied, "Something white and sparkly. If you are dancing, something cool, no long sleeves, but take a wrap or a jacket. Don't take credit cards, wear a body belt or pockets or hang a purse round your neck. It's too easy for people to steal from you in a place like that."

"You're getting me worried."

"No – if you take precautions it can be fun. You like Connor?"

"Very much. He's easy to talk to."

"Don't wear stilettos, they're probably banned and

stick to the same drink so that you can taste if anyone doctors it."

"Will I need ear plugs?"

"Maybe, but you'll definitely need ID."

"I don't have driving licence."

"A passport?"

"Yes, but I'd be scared of losing it."

"Get it photocopied and take the original but keep it with you at all times. Don't worry. You might even enjoy yourself. I must go now."

"Yes, of course. Thank you, Fiona."

Chapter 9

Valerie had selected an orange T shirt with sequins round the neckline, to go with her black leggings and topped it with a white bomber jacket that made her feel ten years younger. She resisted the urge to add hooped earrings, too 1960's, but she did buy a red hair spray to brighten up her hairstyle.

It was odd going out in flat shoes but she didn't want to take a big handbag, instead she had a small shoulder bag that she thought she could keep with her if she danced.

The night club was darker than Valerie had expected. How on earth can people see what they are drinking? she thought. Most of the tables seemed to seat four people but there were some open ended cubicles round the sides with groups of six or more. There seemed to be very little dancing going on, although there were plenty of close encounters.

While Connor went to the bar Valerie sat looking at the other customers. There was nobody there that she recognised, although the age range was considerable. A bunch of teenagers sat round a large table in the corner. Two couples who looked in their fifties shared a table but most of the occupants were in their thirties or forties, she guessed. The music for dancers was eighties disco, with occasional Northern Soul and the odd recognisable pop song. I wonder if they ever play anything slow? Valerie thought. I suppose it's too early.

Connor returned with their drinks and pulled his chair close to hers.

"What do you think?"

"Of the place?"

"Yes."

"It's cleaner than I expected. The music is a bit of a mixture."

He laughed. "People don't take much notice unless there's an act on."

"A singer?"

"Not tonight. Sometimes a comedian and sometimes a drag act. We don't have to stay if you feel uncomfortable." He stretched over and held her hand.

Valerie felt the tension drain from her. When was the last time she had the opportunity to enjoy herself? The throbbing music was enticing. It made her feel like flinging her body around. She couldn't ever remember feeling like this. She took a mouthful of her drink. It was cool and refreshing. She'd let Connor choose for her and he'd brought a long cocktail. She let him lead her away from the table and they began to dance.

They were still on the floor when the music changed and a faster rhythm from Valerie's youth made her smile.

"I know this one," she declared and began to stamp and twirl as she had done years before.

Connor grinned at her and flung his arms in the air, urging her on and she responded, getting more and more uninhibited until she was stepping and twisting and laughing so much she could hardly stay upright. The tune ended and they collapsed into their chairs.

"Another drink, I think." Connor said. "That was great. You really came alive."

"It made me feel good," Valerie said, breathlessly. "But I'm thirsty – something with ice, please, Connor."

"Right you are."

Valerie could feel the perspiration in her hairline. Her heart was racing but she did not want the evening to end.

"Don't they ever play slow numbers?" she asked when he returned with what looked like a large orange juice and lemonade.

"Of course, later on. They know what people like."

"And they like this bouncy stuff first?"

"Yes."

"I'd get indigestion." Valerie giggled, content to make Connor laugh again. He seemed so relaxed in her presence, as if they had known each other for years.

"Where do you come from, Connor?"

"Not Ireland, although my folks were from there. I started off in Liverpool. Then Bristol, then London. I've been moving South all the time. I'm mostly free lance but I cover the odd story for the local rag. They know where I am."

"And Australia?"

"That's just a job. I'm not going to live there."

"What kind of job?"

"Contrasting the town and country – pretty standard stuff, but times change, nothing stays the same and the Brits know so little about the Antipodes."

"Do you ever get political?"

"Not if I can help it. Once you nail your colours to the mast half the publications won't use you. Are you ready to have aother go, now?"

"Once I've found the Ladies,'" Valerie blushed and looked round for a sign.

"By the door where we came in," Connor said. "I'll wait here."

By the time she returned the music had slowed a

little and some of the more energetic dancers had left the floor. Valerie moved into Connor's arms, grateful to be led in a slow smooch. It was comforting to be in a man's arms again and when he whispered in her ear that he thought she was beautiful she felt happier than she had for months. She didn't care what happened next – she was lost in the moment. She was falling in love.

They walked hand in hand to the car and Connor drove them slowly home. "Well, did you like it?" he said when they reached her house.

"Of course I did. It was a wonderful night."

"It's morning now. What are you going to do?"

"I'm going to sleep until lunchtime. I couldn't do this every week."

"Do you want company?"

"Oh, Connor, not tonight, I'm sorry."

"But I can see you again?"

"I'd love that, but when I'm more awake. Do you swim?"

"I do when I get the chance."

"How about the swimming pool? Next Sunday, in the early morning. That's when the pool is almost empty."

"How early?"

"Eight o'clock?"

"Wow. No night club that weekend, then. OK, see you at the pool, 8am Sunday morning. Keep the day free and we'll have a roast lunch."

He reached over to kiss her. It was a little awkward but he managed to connect with her mouth. She wanted to hug him but he was at the wrong angle. He made as if to get out of the car but she motioned for him to stay where he was and opened her door.

"Thanks for a lovely night, Connor."

"See you Sunday, darling," came the reply as he drove away.

"I think I'm a little bit drunk, Bertie," Valerie muttered as she filled a glass with water from the tap. "But he's very special," and, turning off the kitchen light, she staggered up the stairs.

However, once in bed she could not sleep. The feeling of excitement that had overcome her on the dance floor, the sensation of belonging that she had felt in Connor's arms and the thrill of anticipation when she thought of seeing him again kept her awake until daylight forced her to get up and get dressed.

It was ten o'clock when she made her breakfast and there was nothing she felt like doing. It was hot, too hot for gardening. She didn't feel like going to the allotment.

She would write to David. She'd promised to keep in touch after her holiday in the Scillies. She could easily make the events of the previous night amusing. In fact she would email her sister, too – but she would be careful about giving her any idea of how she felt. It was a strange sort of giddiness – a mixture of disbelief and joy. She couldn't think why Connor liked her so much but she felt there was a connection – as if he knew what she was going to say before she said it, that he really cared about what she was thinking and doing, that she mattered to him. Yet that couldn't be true, she thought. He'd only known her a few hours.

"But I'm beginning to feel like that, too," she told Bertie. "I want to make him happy more than anything else in the world. I love making him laugh and I want to be with him all the time. I want to know everything about him and I want him to hold me close so that I can melt into him."

She poured herself a glass of water and, noticing a brown leaf on Bertie's stem, filled a jug and poured some into his pot. "I'm sorry, Bertie. I haven't been looking after you properly," she muttered and went upstairs to write her letters.

"Oi!- none of that!" shouted the lifeguard as Connor grabbed her under the water and dragged her backwards so she was floating in his arms.

"You're a good swimmer," he said.

"And you keep your hands to yourself," Valerie laughed. "No more swimming underwater and through my legs!"

"But they're such lovely legs," Connor responded. "Come on, I'll race you – two lengths."

Valerie beat him easily but his reaction was to carry on laughing. Somehow just being with him made her feel younger, lighter and even when, later, at the restaurant, her yorkshire pudding was soggy and her meat a little tough she didn't care. She was with the man of her dreams and he was treating her as if she was something special.

It was when they were having coffee that Connor reached into his pocket. "I've got you a present. It isn't much, but I saw it and thought of you."

It was a scarf, a delicate scarf with horses, no, not horses, unicorns, white unicorns galloping across a blue sky.

"You remembered," Valerie gasped. "It's beautiful, Connor."

"It's not silk."

"It's perfect. You are spoiling me."

"You make me want to."

Valerie felt a shiver of excitement run through her. There was something about the intensity of his gaze.

She hadn't got anything for him – not yet – unless it was time to invite him to her home. Could she? Was it too soon?

"How about we try the new big wheel on the front?" Connor asked when they came out of the restaurant.

"It doesn't go round too fast?" Valerie asked.

"No. It goes really slowly and gives you a lovely view of the Downs and the sea."

"Have you been on?"

"Not yet. I was waiting for someone to share the experience. Come on. It will be fine."

She looked up at the great wheel and the cubicles hanging from it. It did look quite safe, she thought. It would be another experience to tell her friends about. Connor was certainly introducing her to a new way of looking at life. She smiled happily at him as they entered the pod.

"Just us, in this one," he said and snuggled next to her on the bench.

The wheel turned slowly and she watched as the elegant houses and the busy street seemed to go further away and then turned to look out over the sea. "I didn't realise how many windmills there were out here," she said but had no time to continue as Connor had taken hold of her shoulders and pulled her towards him for a lingering kiss.

Valerie felt her body respond until she was so breathless with her reaction that she had to pull away. "Well, you are a dark horse," Connor commented. "I think I'm falling for you, Val."

"I hope nobody is going to fall," she retorted, trying to calm herself with a joke. "I thought you said we were going to look at the view."

"Don't say you didn't like it." His laughing face

was still inches from hers.

"You've got me all hot and bothered. Now, we're coming near the ground. Behave in public."

"Yes, Miss," he challenged and then waited while the wheel turned and started to rise again.

"How many times does this go round?" Valerie asked.

"Three, and I claim three kisses."

Valerie could not deny him. He had lit a flame of passion in her that she did not want to extinguish.

Once they reached the ground Connor took her arm. "I think we need an ice cream," he said but before they had reached the kiosk his phone rang.

"Yes," Connor snapped and then looked away. He shoved the phone in his pocket and stood up. "I'm sorry, Val. I have to go. It was my paper. There's been an accident near here and they want me to cover it. There's no-one else in the area."

"I understand," Valerie said, meekly, "I hope no-one was hurt."

"I think it was bad. I'd better rush. I'll give you a call. Can you get home all right?"

"Sure. It isn't far. I'll be fine, you go."

So he did, and she was left staring at the queue in front of her.

Now she had two men interested in her but only one who made her feel she did not want to live without him in her life. But did he feel the same? She wasn't sure. She didn't yet know enough about him and he hadn't given her his mobile number. She would have to wait for him to contact her.

Chapter 10

Next weekend she was back at the allotment picking gooseberries and collecting a lettuce and some radishes. She looked at Joe's tomatoes. They were still green and it was too early for potatoes. She was about to leave when Joe arrived, looking harassed.

"Are you OK, Joe?" Valerie asked.

"Yes, I suppose so. The boiler blew up. I've got no hot water. At least it's summer. Did you have a nice holiday?

She felt a shiver of suspicion. Could Joe have had something to do with her burglary? He never seemed to have any money. His clothes were shabby and he needed a haircut. She didn't know who he mixed with when he wasn't at the allotment.

"The holiday was fine but I had a shock when I got home."

"Oh, yes. What was that? Was it to do with the Introduction Agency?"

"No, they were all right. My house had been burgled." She watched carefully to see how he reacted.

"Burgled? Did they take much?"

"All the big saleable items, the TV, the microwave, the music centre."

"Was there much damage?"

"Not a lot- but I still don't feel safe there any more. The police told me to get security lights"

"I'm so sorry, Valerie. I may be able to replace the music centre. Have you still got the CD's?"

"Funnily enough, yes. Maybe they didn't like my choice of music."

"Leave it to me. Were you insured?"

"Yes, but everyone says that takes ages."

"Would you like me to come and see if I can help?"

"I'm still a bit at sixes and sevens- not really up to visitors. They didn't touch the garden, thank goodness." She couldn't tell him she did not trust anyone any more.

"But the police took fingerprints?"

"I think so. I was so upset I didn't see."

"I expect your policeman friend will be useful."

"Mmm," Valerie didn't reveal that she had not yet told Richard. Her time at the allotment had been ruined by her suspicions. Was there anywhere she could relax? She began to think she might consider moving – but first she had to get herself organised enough to go to work.

Just leaving the house to go up to London was going to be a wrench, but Judy had said she would keep a look out and she had new locks on the back entrances. She hadn't bought an alarm. She thought those boxes made the houses look as if there was something valuable inside. I've got nothing valuable left, she thought.

Valerie was struggling to understand the controls of her new television. It was very frustrating. Every time she tried to change channels she had to check that she was on the right button on the remote or she hit the timer and lost the picture altogether.

"I will learn it," she declared to Bertie as she retreated to the kitchen. "I don't need a man to show me how to use a TV."

It was still a relief when the phone rang and Richard's voice came over the line.

"Hallo, Richard. Nice to hear from you."

"I'm glad about that. I have some news."

"You've met someone else?"

Richard laughed. "Not exactly. Can we meet? I would like to see you again."

"You'd like me to come swimming?"

"That would be ideal."

"But no funny business?"

"I'll be on my best behaviour – how about next Saturday?"

"I'm not sure, Richard. So much has happened since I saw you last."

"And to me. I'll expect you at ten."

"I'll look forward to it."

As she put the phone down Valerie realised she had been telling the truth. She could trust Richard. She was aware of his faults. He didn't pretend to be anything other than himself. Why couldn't she feel attracted to him?

Richard opened the door to his flat with a beaming smile on his face.

"You look like the cat that got the cream," Valerie remarked.

"I have. I've been promoted – no longer a sergeant, behold, Inspector Stillman. But there's one catch. I'll be stationed at Horsham. No more runs on the beach and more travelling than I'm used to."

"You're happy, though?"

"Jolly happy. In fact I'm going to buy a new car to celebrate."

"You'll keep the flat?"

"For the time being. I'd miss the facilities. Have you brought your costume?"

"Yes, and a towel. I'm ready when you are."

Richard was a powerful swimmer but Valerie was

quick and the pair had an enjoyable time in the pool. When they came out Richard offered her soup or salad.

"It's too warm for soup," Valerie said. "Can I do anything to help?"

"No, it's all prepared. I just need to add the tomatoes. Everyone says they shouldn't be kept in the fridge,"

"You make me feel really sloppy. Don't say you made the quiche, too?"

"Sorry to disappoint you. M and S best, I'm afraid."

"What is Horsham like?"

"Mixed, like most places. Nice shops and beautiful countryside, but odd patches of problem housing and a few nasties from London. There was a smash and grab there last week. A jewellers."

Valerie hadn't meant to tell him about her break in but she blurted out, "I was robbed last month."

"Robbed, when, how? Were you hurt?"

"No, not robbed personally, just the house, while I was away."

"That's burglary, not robbery."

"It's all the same to me."

"What did they steal?"

"The TV, the music centre, the microwave, some jewellery. I didn't have anything valuable."

"I didn't hear about that. Someone will be in trouble for not telling me."

"I expect you had other things on your mind."

"True. I should have checked the crime list for your area. I usually do. Who came round?"

"A policeman and a policewoman. I forget their names. They said to fix the door and get a security light."

"Funny that, your street doesn't look very affluent, what with being so near the railway."

"We aren't. Someone must have known I would be away."

"Maybe some of the stuff will show up in Brighton, although it's usually got rid of in pubs. Have you got to get home for anything special?"

"No, I'm in to work on Monday but I'm a free agent over the weekend. In fact I don't like being in the house on my own any more."

"How would you like to come and look at cars with me?"

"I don't know anything about cars."

"I can choose what I want by what's under the bonnet but you can tell me if it's comfortable and the right colour."

"I don't like black."

"That's one decision made, then. Strawberries and cream and then we'll go car hunting!"

When they reached the garage Valerie discovered that Richard had actually made an appointment. He knew exactly what make of car he wanted, a Volvo, and he encouraged her to sit in one in the showroom. It was silver and she didn't think it was the colour she would have associated with him. The salesman showed them images of different models and she watched Richard's eyes. When he saw the red car his lips lifted into a smile.

"What do you think, Valerie?" he asked.

"You want the car we saw in silver?"

"Yes. Did you find it comfortable?"

"Perfect, but I think the red is more you." Richard's face broke into a broad grin.

"That's exactly what I thought. They do it in red, don't they?" he said to the salesman.

"Yes, although we don't have one here. It will take a couple of weeks. Would you like to choose a number plate?"

"Sure, and we'll have to sort out a price for the Golf."

"If you'll come this way. Would you like tea, coffee?"

"I'd like a glass of water, please," said Valerie.

Once the details were settled the salesman said, "Would you like a trial run in the model we have here?"

"I did have a go last week," Richard admitted, "but you'd like a run, wouldn't you, Valerie?"

"I'd love it."

The ride was as smooth and the feeling as luxurious as she had expected. Richard was a confident driver although she was a little disconcerted when he swore at another car that cut in front of them and made him brake. Maybe I ought to learn to drive? she thought. If I could do that I could think about moving. Her house no longer seemed a sanctuary. Whatever she did to it she'd never feel content.

Of course, if she found a man she wanted to live with for the rest of her life it wouldn't have mattered, but, so far, she had been out of luck. Then she remembered the allotment. She wouldn't want to give that up. She needed to be a local resident to keep it. If she moved, it wouldn't have to be far away.

Chapter 11

Valerie sat on the train on Monday morning making a list. First, she would make an effort to find a job nearer home. She wouldn't get London weighting but she'd save on the fares.

Then she'd look for a flat near the allotments. There were some mock Georgian ones that overlooked the park or, if not, some more modern ones near the Leisure Centre.

She'd get someone to value her house and book some driving lessons. It was a newly invigorated Valerie who turned up at work full of stories about her holiday but determined to look forward, not back.

Valerie had chosen a lady driving instructor. She was tired of the complications that meeting new men had involved. It was still summer so she could have one lesson in the week and she booked another for Sundays. There would be no time, for a while, to make new connections.

Valerie paused in the doorway of the Estate Agent's.

There were three desks spaced across the room, one to her left, one to her right, one further back.

The desk to the left of her had a woman smiling and asking "Can I help you?" while the one to her right had a man who looked serious but alert.

Valerie chose left and sat down, taking the outstretched hand as she did so.

"I'm thinking of selling my house." she began. "I'd like it valued, please."

"Could you give us the address?"

Valerie did so-and watched as the estate agent punched a few buttons and brought up her street on the computer in front of her.

"Which day would suit you, Mrs?"

"Davies, Valerie Davies – any evening after seven or at weekends by arrangement."

"Our valuer, Tony, could be with you on Friday evening. Is that any good to you?"

"Oh, that's really quick." Valerie had visions of herself trying to tidy up and clean the place before the visit.

"The following week, then? How about Tuesday?"

"That would be better."

She returned home feeling that she was finally in charge of her own destiny. I must look forward, not back, she thought, echoing David's advice.

Valerie tried to look at the house as if she was a purchaser. What would they notice? They should discount the furniture but the walls, were they a popular colour? Some were painted and some had wallpaper. Was there enough light? Valerie liked blinds in the kitchen but curtains in the other rooms.

What should she do with Bertie? She couldn't move him on her own. He was too heavy. Besides, he was a feature. He made her kitchen feel different. She sprayed water on his leaves. "Goodness knows how I'll move you when the time comes." she told him.

She didn't expect to hear that the intruders had been caught and she was correct. Richard said that her jewellery could turn up at a pawnbrokers. No-one had seen the burglars so they couldn't be identified. "We'll get them – when they do it again," was Richard's attitude.

Meanwhile she had been pleasantly surprised by the valuation of her home. Even without a garage it was more than she had expected and she had seen some flats on line that looked promising although the idea of having a lease instead of a freehold did concern her a little. She knew landlords tended to put up maintenance charges. That would be manageable while she was working but not once she was a pensioner.

It wasn't long before she began to get enquiries about the house and had to arrange viewings. The first prospective buyers were a young couple who said they had a baby who was staying with her grandmother while they looked at property in the area.

"This will be our first home," the young woman said as they stood in the bedroom, looking down at the street below.

"Not necessarily," said her husband. "We have two other viewings this week."

Turning to Valerie he asked , "What's the area like? Much crime?"

Valerie couldn't reply. If she told them about the burglary they would never buy the house, and nor would anyone else. Yet the area was quiet. Nobody else had been targeted and she had updated her security.

"I suppose it's the same as everywhere else, nowadays," she said, "and I've got good locks and a security light. It's better to take precautions."

"I guess being at the end of a row makes you more vulnerable."

"Maybe, but it's nice to be able to get into the garden from the side. Would you like to see the garden?"

"You go, darling. Gardens aren't really my thing. I'll stay here if that's OK?" He took out his phone as if he was going to use it..

The two women went out through the kitchen and

stood looking at her garden.

"It's beautiful, and so neat," said the young woman when they stood outside. "But we'd have to change it, get rid of the raised beds and the greenhouse. We want a big lawn and a patio. Kevin wants to make it a playground for Josie."

"How old is your little one?"

"Nearly two, but he dotes on her. Have you got any children?"

"No, that's why the little bedroom is an office. My husband died a while ago so it doesn't look likely now, does it?"

"I'm sorry. Are you moving anywhere local?"

"I'm not sure. I just thought I didn't need all this space."

"You've kept it very nice."

"Thank you."

On their return indoors Kevin met them in the hallway.

"Thank you, Mrs Davies ," he said. "We'll have to discuss it, won't we, darling?"

"What? Oh, yes, I'm sure we'll be in touch. Thank you for showing us round."

Valerie could see the husband couldn't wait to get away. She wondered what had put him off. He obviously hadn't felt at home. Perhaps it felt too feminine. There was no sign of a man in the house. More likely it was the fact that she didn't have a garage. The street was filled with parked cars. There weren't many young couples who didn't own a vehicle these days.   She was suddenly very tired. Was she trying to change too much, too soon? Should she just relax and let her life drift on as usual? Not having anyone to talk things over with was wearing her out.

It had been so different with James. He had made

her feel that she was half of a whole, that they needed to be together for balance, like a boat with two oars. It was a feeling she missed, desperately. Somehow she just couldn't see Richard as a confidante and she didn't even know when Connor would contact her again. Perhaps I'll feel different as we get to know each other better, she thought.

Chapter 12

When she got off the bus in town the next day Connor was waiting for her.

"I've something to tell you," he said. "Let's find somewhere to sit down."

"You're going away?"

"No – the opposite. I've turned down the job in Australia. I couldn't bear the thought of being away from you. I'll just order us some tea, shall I?"

"Oh, Connor. I'm sorry," Valerie said when he returned with the teas.

"Don't be. I have another assignment. I have to write about the High Streets of Britain. It means travelling all over the country and comparing towns, seeing how they are coping with the latest retail trends, on line shopping and business rates. It will be really interesting."

"But you have to leave?"

"Not yet. First I want to take you somewhere special – somewhere you'd like. Have you ever been to the Lavender Farm?"

"No, it's somewhere I wanted to visit but we never got there."

"I'd like to take you. How about next Saturday? They do cream teas. It would be a lovely day out."

"I'd love it." She grasped his hand. "You spoil me."

He smiled. "It might make a good article for one of the gardening magazines."

"You crafty thing. I did wonder if it was really your kind of date. Now I understand."

"You'll be with me. What more could I want? Now, I must be off. I can't stop now. There's someone I have to see. Ten thirty next Saturday?"

"I'll be waiting. Thanks, Connor." She drank her cooling tea on her own.

Valerie found it almost impossible to keep the proposed trip to herself. She had looked up the lavender fields on the internet but was very aware that Connor could be called away on another job at any time and not be able to take her.

Then, when Saturday came and he didn't arrive at ten thirty she began to get alarmed. Surely he would call her if he was going to be late? What if he had had an accident? She was about to panic when his car drew up and he got out, looking flushed but otherwise intact.

"Oh. Connor." she said. "I was getting worried."

"It's all fixed," he said. "The car was playing up but I sorted it. We're good to go."

"At least it's sunny, but I'm not sure it will last."

"No matter, the tour is before the tea. We should be indoors by the time the rain reaches us."

They stopped for a burger and lemonade at a transport cafe where to Valerie's dismay they were surrounded by bikers. How was Connor to know that James had ridden a bike and she had a sharp reminder of her younger self, riding pillion through the countryside? It seemed like another Valerie, another time and she pushed the memory away. She was determined not to let the past spoil the present.

She couldn't help giggling to herself as they were taken round the lavender fields. It did remind her a little of the time she was introduced to the vineyard but this time, instead of buying wine, they were supposed to take home oils or soaps or lavender infused pillows.

Connor was in his element, taking photographs and quizzing the guide about the history of the place.

As they stood together looking over the ocean of purple blooms Valerie said, "Isn't it magnificent? It must feel like this when you go to the tulip fields in Holland."

"We'll go there one day," responded Connor, nuzzling her ear and she couldn't remember ever being so content.

The cream tea was delicious, although Valerie wasn't quite so keen on lavender biscuits. By five o'clock they were ready to set off home.

Then the rains came.

"I can't see well enough to drive in this," said Connor. "How about we stop somewhere for an early dinner?"

"I won't need much but this is no fun," replied Valerie.

"OK, the next likely place. There's loads of country pubs on this route."

Ten minutes later they were driving into the car park of a hotel advertising a restaurant.

"Let's hope it's not too busy on a Saturday night." Connor said as they raced towards the large double doors.

"I'm not dressed for fine dining," laughed Valerie.

"We'll have a bar meal. They won't turn us out in this."

In fact the restaurant was only half full and they were shown to a secluded table in the corner and handed menus by a young waitress with a shy smile.

"It's rather expensive," said Valerie.

"Don't fret. This is a treat. Goodness only knows when we'll have another day like today. Push the boat out."

Valerie studied the menu. What did she feel like? "I'd like the quiche with salad, please, Connor."

"Right, I'll have the fish and we can share a bottle of Pino Grigio. Dessert?"

"There's raspberry pavlova. Do you think we could share one?"

Connor laughed. "You are being careful, aren't you? You don't have to watch your weight, you know."

"I just don't feel like a lot. I think it's the excitement."

She couldn't interpret the sideways glance he gave her but he gave the order and they settled back for a companionable meal.

It was dark when they finished and Connor went outside to check on the car.

"Bad news, I'm afraid. She won't start. I think it's the same problem as I had this morning. I thought a good run would fix it but it hasn't. We'll have to get a taxi, or stay the night."

"But I don't have anything with me."

"I have a spare hoodie and a clean toothbrush in the boot. What else do you need? I'll ask if they have any rooms."

How strange, thought Valerie, but then he is used to being called out to go anywhere at any time. It did seem as if they were fated to spend the night together - but how together? If there was only one room, one bed, should she refuse and demand a taxi? What did she really want?

Connor came back shaking his head. "All they have is one double room," he said. "I don't want to upset you."

"You think sharing a room with you would upset me?" responded Valerie. "Don't you know how I feel about you?"

"Well I hoped, but I didn't want to rush you. I've had such a job keeping my hands off you. Would you really share a bed?"

"Connor, I think I'd like to spend the rest of my life with you. If you feel the same, let's start tonight."

"You lovely, lovely woman. You have just made me the happiest man in the world."

"Then let's look at this room. If it's a dump I'll change my mind."

It wasn't a dump. It was warm and beautifully furnished with an en-suite bathroom and a soft and inviting king sized bed.

"Connor, there's bathrobes behind the door as well as towels and a choice of soaps and shampoos.

This is like a palace. Can I have a bath?"

"You do that. I'll use the shower when you've finished. I'll just go down and ring my garage – see if they can get the car fixed for us to go back tomorrow. If not I'll try a mate.It might not be easy on a Sunday."

She couldn't remember ever being so nervous as she prepared to go to bed with Connor. She was glad he had left her long enough for her to dry herself and slip between the sheets. She hadn't wanted to be naked so she was still wearing the fluffy white bathrobe, although she knew it was stupid.

He didn't say anything when he returned but came out of the bathroom, also wearing a robe, after his shower. "I see you opened the toothbrush," he said. "We'll have to share."

"It's a comfy bed," she remarked,

"Am I invited in?"

"Of course."

He flung his robe aside and climbed in beside her. "My feet are cold," she apologised.

"Well the rest of you can't be," he chided and rolled her bathrobe over one shoulder.

She couldn't help herself. She wriggled out of the robe and dropped it onto the floor. She'd never made love in the nude before and felt as if she wanted to squeeze herself next to him from her neck to her toes.

He put his arm across the pillows and stroked her hair.

It was as if he made her melt. He bent towards her and gently kissed her breasts. It was almost too much to bear but it was when he stopped to talk she realised this was going to be like no love making she had ever experienced.

Not only did Connor talk, he actually asked her how she felt, he waited to see what effect his words and actions were having on her. "What would you like, my love?" he asked, sitting astride her and grasping her wrists, pulling them above her head so that she felt like a prisoner. "This?"

The urgent pain she felt was delicious agony. Her breath was coming in short, sharp gasps.

"Or this?" he asked and, letting go of her arms pushed his head between her legs,

"Don't," she cried, feebly, not meaning it, as she began to burn with desire. Connor laughed and lay full length on top of her. "You're beautiful." he said. "I want you so much."

"Please, please," she said and her back arched as he fondled her.

"Are you ready for me?"

"Yes, yes," and at last he gave her what her body was craving.

When she got home next day the answer machine was flashing so she picked up the receiver.

"You had your mobile turned off," Fiona grumbled.

"Yes, I went away for the weekend so I left it at home. Is there a problem?"

"I believe so. Were you with Connor Fields?"

"Yes, why?"

"Someone came into the office yesterday to complain about him."

"Complain -how?"

"She said he had deceived her; that he was married. She was on holiday here and she spotted him coming out of our office. She said he'd promised to marry her but when he found out she didn't own her own home he broke off the engagement. She didn't even have a ring."

"Are you sure it was Connor?" Valerie said not wanting to believe it was true. She had felt a connection, been ready to accept him into her life, even begun to wonder what their children would look like. She had slept well and they had enjoyed a full English breakfast. It had felt like a honeymoon. He'd been so attentive, so interested in her, so ready to please her. Their journey home in a friend's car had been cosy and he had promised to be in touch as soon as he knew when his next job started.

She had been in such a romantic daze that it wasn't until they were nearing her house that it occurred to her that he hadn't used any protection the previous night.

"I'm sorry, Valerie. We had no idea," continued Fiona. "She knew exactly what he would have told us. His story checked out. The only part that was true was that he was a reporter. He works for a paper in

Hastings but when she asked for him they were very cagey so she rang again and said she was his wife. They were completely different and told her he was on a job but they'd pass on a message. We can only do so much. We'll do better next time, I promise you."

Valerie put the phone down. She clutched at her body as if the pain was physical. She couldn't speak as the tears fell. He'd been so sweet, so loving, so special. It couldn't be true. Perhaps he had been deceiving other women but he could not have been cheating her. Could he? She thought over everything that had happened. Had his car really broken down? Had he planned to spend the night with her all along? What was he going to say to her next time they met – if ever they did meet again? What if he had made her pregnant?

Her tears were tears of anger as much as disappointment. She was angry at herself for allowing him to deceive her, angry at him for being such a cheat and angry at fate for turning hope into disaster. I don't deserve this, she thought. I'll never trust anyone again.

It wasn't rape, was it? They were what is called 'consenting adults.' No – what had happened to her was seduction. She laughed bitterly at the word, associated as it was with historical romances. Well, it still happened, didn't it – and it had happened to her!

In a perverse way she was happy that she had had the experience but her overwhelming feeling was hurt. Connor had deceived her, used her. She hadn't mattered to him. He had made her fall in love with him and not cared.

Even his present of a scarf with the unicorns seemed symbolic, now. After all, they were mythical. She couldn't rip it up but she folded it into the bottom of a drawer. It would always remind her of how gullible she had been.

To think she had even begun to imagine what being married to him would be like. They would have a quiet registry office wedding and live in her house until they found something that would be their choice. She had visions of helping him with his work, showing him over the allotment, introducing him to all her friends.

Now, if he'd made her pregnant, she would be in disgrace. Everyone would know how foolish she had been. Her parents would be horrified and her friends would probably treat her differently, if they did not abandon her.

She'd stayed awake at night wondering if she could cope, imagining how having a child would change her life, worrying if she would love it or hate it. She never wanted to see Connor again but would she have to ask him for money? Could she pretend she didn't know the father? What would people think of her then?

Now she would have to act as if she didn't care that he was no longer in her life. She had made so many mistakes and had so many unhappy experiences that she could not go on as she had done. She had tried to find someone to share her life but it was more difficult than she had expected. She would have to find other ways of satisfying her craving for change. She would put to the back of her mind the possibility that she might be a single mother.

Chapter 13

It was a re-energised Valerie who entered the estate agent's determined to take control of her own life. The headache that had been her consant companion for days had vanished and it was as if she could see clearly at last. She had finally had the sign that her body was behaving as normal. She was not expecting Connor's baby. The relief made her even more determined to change her life.

Now she had made the decision to move house she had begun to imagine what it would be like in a smaller, more compact home – one that she could furnish and decorate to suit herself, and she was hopeful that it wouldn't take too long.

However, once she had stated her requirements she discovered that it wasn't going to be that easy.

The estate agent gave her details of two flats and suggested she view them as soon as possible as they did not stay on the market for very long.

The first was in a large block near the sea but the vacant flat was on the third floor and there were only communal gardens. She hadn't realised that having to press a security button to get through the front door and ride up to her home in a lift would make her feel uncomfortable. She didn't need to see round the place to know that it wasn't what she wanted.

The next option appeared to be almost all she had hoped for. It was a ground floor maisonette, with a completely different feel about it. It had its own front door, which was really at the back of the property where the paved area held rotary clothes lines and the garages and a communal front garden which was a large lawn surrounded by low shrubs.

"There's a regular gardener but tenants are allowed to put pot plants under their windows if they are on the ground floor," the agent explained. "It's supposed to be a sitting out area but as it faces the road it's rarely used as such."

"It faces west," Valerie mused, "It must get the sun in the morning. I wonder if we could have a bird bath on the grass?"

It was going to need a new style of thinking to share a garden. It was a good job she had half an allotment to experiment in.

The narrow hallway had a door to the right which opened on to a large bedroom. To the left was the bathroom. The room at the end was a long L shaped room serving as a kitchen, a dining room and a lounge, with two balconied windows looking out over the park. I'd have to get a laptop, thought Valerie, there's no room for an office.

Could she be happy here? she wondered. She supposed it depended on who her neighbours were, especially the people upstairs. It was very quiet and the maisonettes were so small she doubted if any were occupied by children.

"I'd need to have a survey," Valerie ventured, "but I haven't sold my house yet."

"That could be a problem, but I'll let the seller know if you are willing to make an offer of the full asking price."

"I don't know. I don't like being rushed. Can I call you later in the week?"

"Of course."

I could see myself there, Valerie thought, but I would have to get rid of so much and I might be just as lonely. She would miss Judy and the garden she had turned into an oasis for birds, bees and butterflies.

"I'd have to grow lavender and rosemary in pots," she grumbled to Bertie as she made her supper, "and there's no buddleia, just a low box hedge round a lawn. I wish I knew if I was doing the right thing."

Just staring at her precious plant calmed her. 'Wait and see if you can sell this house, first,' he seemed to advise.

She sat at the kitchen table with a poached egg on toast and a pot of tea. The optimism she had felt while viewing the little maisonette was draining away. Wherever she lived she was still going to be on her own.

Some people manage quite happily, she thought, but it's making me old before my time. I want to create, not hibernate, and she gave a bitter laugh at the unintentional rhyme.

Sorting her stuff for the move was more upsetting than she could ever have imagined. She felt disloyal to James to be moving out of the home they had purchased together

"I do hope he'd understand," she told Bertie. "I can't stay here. I don't feel safe." But there was so much she had to throw away. She'd got used to having two reception rooms and a kitchen she could spend time in. She would be restricted to a tiny kitchen area and a 'through' room. James's chair would have to go. She wouldn't leave Bertie behind. He would have pride of place by the window.

Not only had she put in an offer for her prospective new home by September, but she had also given in her notice and found a position in a shop in Chichester.

"It has new owners," she told Richard, "but I don't think they are going to close it down or they wouldn't be recruiting staff. It will be so much easier just travelling along the coast to work."

"You'll be in with the posh crowd," Richard replied.

"No posher than London. Besides, I still have my friends at the allotment. At least, I think they are still my friends." She tried not to imagine Joe as a burglar. After all, they had shared the spinach, potatoes, sweetcorn and blackcurrants on their patch, but their easy intimacy had gone and she didn't know how to get it back. I'll not rest until I know who robbed me, she thought.

It was late October when Richard surprised her with an invitation.

"I'd like you to partner me at the force's Christmas dinner- dance, Valerie."

"When is it?"

"The first Saturday in December."

"And there's no-one else you can ask?" she teased.

"You know there isn't, and I might have some good news for you."

"Oh, yes? What?"

"Your music centre turned up in a shop we had our eye on and we have a glimpse of the man who brought it in. He's not known to us but we circulated his picture. It's just the lead we needed."

"He's not a known criminal, then?"

"No, but we think we can trace him through his vehicle. It's an old car."

"It makes me shudder to think of it. I thought I'd got over the shock. I won't have to go to court, will I?"

"I doubt it. You didn't see anything, or get hurt. Let's just wait and see. I wouldn't be surprised if he hadn't done other jobs – with other people. We may be able to link him to some other unsolved cases."

"I expect you need to find where he stores the things he steals?"

"Yes. It will be a garage or a shed somewhere. Still, forget him. I want to give you your Christmas present early."

"Oh, Richard, why?" He produced a small box.

I hope it isn't an engagement ring, Valerie thought as he opened the lid. Inside was a locket on a silver chain.

"Please say you like it. It's to make up for all your lost jewellery."

"It's beautiful, Richard. I'll wear it at the dinner."

"That's what I hoped you'd say," and he folded her into his arms.

"I tried to relax," she told Bertie, "but I think I'm a little bit scared of him. He does sometimes lose his temper, especially when he's driving. It makes my tummy turn over." She knew she ought to tell Richard how she felt but she didn't want to annoy him. Instead she had to search for an appropriate present for him, and find a photo to put in the locket. He'd already put his own portrait in one side. She wasn't sure she liked that. It was another sign of the possessiveness that had alarmed her when they first met. Meanwhile was there something for his car she could buy, or something to wear? She'd look on line for something special, decorative but not romantic, like cuff links; there was plenty of choice.

It was fun looking at all the different designs, knots and golf clubs, planes and stripes, but in the end she chose a round silver set with a lapis lazuli centre. It was a rich blue and she liked the simplicity of it.

Chapter 14

Her next trip to the allotment saw her taking a fresh look at Joe's hut. It was bigger than her little tool shed that they had turned into a lean to and she thought she had never seen all of the inside. She'd been happy to let him make tea and feed her biscuits.

Could she trust him – or was he the person who had instigated her burglary? It had been a busy few weeks and she had been involved with the house sale and the new job so she hadn't had time to sit and chat. She wanted to tell him about Richard's invitation but hesitated to bring up the subject. She felt awkward around him and all his efforts to rekindle their previous camaraderie failed.

Should she try to see what was inside his hut? Could she be that deceitful? He'd been a good friend and now their relationship was ruined. The only way to be sure it wasn't him was to investigate. She would not be content until she knew for certain that he hadn't been the burglar.

Joe was sitting in his hut when she arrived, mending a broken spade.

"Too much digging with too ancient tools," he explained. "I think I need some new ones."

"Can't you fix it?"

"Not permanently. I got a bit carried away. Now my back aches and I can't finish the row. I'm afraid it won't get dug before the frosts."

"Oh, Joe. It's ages before that happens."

"Trust you to look on the bright side. How's things?"

"I've had an invitation."

"From Richard?

"Yes, to a dinner dance."

"Ah – the Policeman's Ball. Did you accept?"

"I did, but I'm a bit nervous."

"Don't be, you'd be an asset wherever you went."

"Stop it, you've only seen me when I'm not bothered how I look."

"You always look good to me. Have a cuppa?"

"I'd love one. It's a bit chilly."

She sat on the garden chair he pulled up to the table and tried to think how to distract him.

"What kind of car is yours?"

"A Skoda. People laugh at them but they're very reliable."

"I'm learning to drive, Joe."

"You are? Wonderful."

"You don't have a copy of the highway code, do you?"

"Not an up to date one. I have the old version in the car. Would you like to borrow it?"

"It would do until I got a new one, wouldn't it?"

"Maybe, but there's lots of new rules. I didn't have to do the theory test."

"Lucky you."

"I'll just fetch it. Have a biscuit," and he moved the tin towards her.

Valerie waited until he was out of sight and then got up and pushed at the door at the rear of the hut. At first it seemed to resist, then, as she pushed harder it opened a crack. There was no window and it was very dark but she could see in the gloom there were sets of shelves on each side. On the floor were bags of compost and along the walls were tins of paint, insecticide, fertilizer and weedkiller. There was no sign of any stolen goods. She gave a sigh of relief. It didn't look as if Joe was the thief after all. She pulled the door shut.

"Here you go," Joe said, handing her the booklet, "and if you want extra practice I'd be glad to take you out sometime."

"Thanks, Joe – maybe when I've had more lessons," Valerie replied and gave him a broad smile. "How would you like some of my blackcurrant jam next time I come?"

"You're a treasure," Joe responded.

Valerie's new job in the finance department of the store in Chichester included customer complaints and it took some time to adapt to the extra responsibility.

"It's more interesting than just figures," she told Judy, "but I have to be diplomatic and careful about what I put in writing."

"How's the sale, going?" Judy asked.

"It's difficult when I am only here weekends and evenings. The agent says it's the wrong time of year. I was gazumped on the flat I wanted because I hadn't sold my house. I might have to wait until Spring."

"Good," Judy replied. "I didn't want you to move."

Valerie laughed. "I think I'll need somewhere with a garage. I'm going to start looking for a car of my own. My instructor says I'm nearly ready for my test. That's the next thing on the agenda."

"What are you doing for Christmas?"

"I don't want to think about it – but I do have a dance to go to with Richard."

"How lovely. What are you wearing?"

"Something new – would you like to help me choose?"

"I'd love to – this Saturday? I could come in the afternoon."

"Fine. I'll look locally and if I can't find anything I'll look in Chichester. Thanks, Judy. It will be fun."

Next day she had a letter from a customer that disturbed her more than most. Instead of the usual complaints about late delivery, the wrong colour, shape, size etc this was a complicated story about a settee.

Apparently the item in question, a brown three seater settee, had been delivered to a Mrs Margaret Salt by the employees of the store who then offered to get rid of her old sofa for a small fee. It didn't have any labels with fire protection so she couldn't give it to charity. She'd been so grateful she had given them twenty pounds and thought no more about it.

However, a week later she had a letter from the Council. While clearing an illegal rubbish dump they had come across her sofa which, unfortunately, had an envelope stuffed down the side with her name and address, 'a habit I had of tucking unwanted advertising catalogues when I had a pile of post,' she had written. 'Please can you find out who the delivery drivers were? I cannot afford to pay a fine for something I haven't done. Besides, they may do it to someone else.'

Valerie sighed. This was more than she could handle on her own. She would have to approach the manager. How many delivery drivers did they have? She had the name and address of the complainant but no date of delivery. Maybe she could do a little preliminary investigation of her own?

At lunch she asked the order clerk if they had records of which drivers took items to which addresses on specific dates.

"Why do you want to know?"

"A customer wants to get in touch with one of

them."

"Is it a complaint?"

"I think she lost something and she hopes he might have found it."

"Well, come to my office this afternoon after work and I'll check it out."

Valerie explained the situation and was directed to the supervisor.

"Leave it with me," was the curt reply when she had offered the letter. Valerie had stopped herself giving an opinion. She went home without visiting the delivery department.

She would try to put it out of her mind. There were more enjoyable things to think about.

Chapter 15

"Do you know what colour you want?" Judy asked when she and Valerie got off the bus in town.

"I'd love to find a long dress in kingfisher blue," Valerie replied, "but if it isn't this season's colour I'll probably be unlucky."

"Well, we've two shops to start with," her friend said. "Shall we start with the nearest one?

"OK, but I'm after something special. I'm not going to scrimp on the price."

"Lucky you."

The ladies' department in the first store they tried had nothing in kingfisher blue but they did find a black dress that fitted Valerie perfectly.

"That's your style," Judy said.

"Yes. I didn't want anything off the shoulder. I don't like wearing a bra with no straps."

"How about the gold one?"

"Too flashy. That just isn't me."

"OK, let's try over the road."

Once again there was nothing that fitted Valerie in kingfisher. She was beginning to get despondent when the assistant brought out a long red dress with lace sleeves and a wide boat neckline.

"That's different," Judy said. "Try it on."

"I don't think I'm really 'the lady in red' type," Valerie said, "but it does look special."

"How can you look demure and sexy all at the same time?" Judy remarked.

Valerie looked at herself in the mirror. She hadn't considered sleeves, or red, but it suited her. In fact she felt wonderful in it.

"I can't believe it," she said, "It changes me."

"No, it doesn't. You're just seeing what other people see," Judy replied, "A cracker."

"I need more make-up."

"And a handbag."

"I've got red shoes at home."

"There, you were meant to have it."

"You know, I think I was."

Valerie was still wondering how she could live up to the image portrayed by the red dress when Richard arrived to pick her up.

"Wow!" he said when she opened the front door. "You look stunning."

"It's not too much?"

"It's beautiful. I'll have the best looking date in the room."

"Do I need to bring anything?" Valerie asked, feeling flustered.

"It would be a pity to cover up that lovely dress but we might be late."

"I've only got a cream stole. It won't rain, will it?"

"Let's risk it."

He took her hand and led her towards the car, opening the passenger door with a flourish.

"Stop it," Valerie giggled. "You're making us a show."

"And why not? We're out to enjoy ourselves."

It was encouraging to find him in such an ebullient mood. Valerie sat back determined not to let anything spoil the evening.

With a choice of chicken, fish or the vegetarian option Valerie decided to have the aubergine with mushroom stuffing.

True to form, Richard selected the chicken pie.

"White wine?" he asked.

"Yes, please."

They were at a table for six and he introduced her to their companions but they all seemed older than her and knew each other well enough to joke and laugh together. The men seemed to spend much of their time playing golf and the women talked to each other across her. The man on her left did try to start a conversation, asking her where she met Richard, but this was a question she did not feel at liberty to answer honestly. She looked at Richard for help.

"Valerie's a swimmer," Richard answered. "She uses the pool in my block of flats."

Valerie smiled at him gratefully and turned back to her neighbour. "Are you based in Horsham , too?"

"No, I'm in Brighton, and Tom over there is at HQ. Steve's the only Horsham one here, and Sally, she's in the force, too. What's your line of business?"

"I'm in the finance department of a store in Chichester – nothing exciting."

"But Chichester is a nice town," his wife chipped in. "I always like going there."

"It's very different from Brighton," Valerie began, but the woman had turned away. The policeman gave an apologetic smile. "Do you live in Brighton?" he asked.

"No, a few miles along the coast." For some reason she did not want to tell him too much.

"Pity," he said , and then paused as someone rose to announce the speeches.

"I'll not talk for long," said the Chief Constable. "I know you are all waiting for the raffle but I want to congratulate you for another year when, in spite of cuts, our figures show another improvement and our detection rate is up."

"Not in my case," Valerie muttered.

"Shh, I've some news about that," Richard said. "I think we've recovered some of your stuff."

"You know who did it?"

"We know who tried to sell it."

"What?"

"The TV. It turned up at a boot sale in Hove. The thieves aren't very bright. I'll tell you more after the raffle. Here. I got five quids worth of tickets," and he spread them out across the table.

Valerie hadn't noticed the pile of prizes on the tables along the side wall and when she looked she realised every gift had a number.

"It's a 'get what you're given' raffle?"

"Yes, it's quicker. You don't have to get up. They bring the prize to you."

"But you never get to choose."

"No, but everything's pretty valuable. There's no rubbish."

She watched, amazed, as the prizes were distributed, bottles of spirits, boxes of chocolates, biscuits, bedding, pot plants, sets of wine glasses and cutlery, even a large jigsaw puzzle and an enormous fluffy white polar bear.

The man sitting next to her won a Christmas tree with illuminations and one of the wives won a box of crackers.

When Richard's ticket was called she waited nervously to see what they had won. It was a long, thin envelope and Richard handed it to her to open.

"It's from a hotel," Valerie said. "It's a weekend away, three nights in a five star hotel, oh Richard!"

"Fabulous," he replied, unaware of her reaction. "I couldn't have picked a better prize."

But Valerie was struggling to look pleased when all she wanted to do was scream, "No, no, can I have a pot plant, instead!"

She felt like a cheat and a liar. She'd almost convinced herself that Richard was the man for her and now, in a flash of clarity she realised she didn't love him and did not want to spend the rest of her life with him. She had been pretending that their friendship might blossom into something more, pretending to herself and him, so that he had assumed that, in time, they would be a couple.

She needed to get him on his own and confess. She knew he would be hurt and wondered if he would be able to control himself when she told him. Could she do it tonight or must she let him have this one evening of happy anticipation? He looked so satisfied- as if all his dreams had come true. How could she destroy that?

"Let's dance," Richard whispered in her ear and she let herself be guided onto the dance floor. Richard was an excellent dancer and if she hadn't been so tense she would have enjoyed being in his arms. He was humming to the music and pulling her close.

"You smell nice," he said.

"Can we sit down? I've got something for you."

He held her arm as they returned to the table and she reached into her bag.

"It's your Christmas present. You don't have to open it now. Keep it for the day."

"Not on your nelly. I want to see what it is," and he unwrapped the little parcel and took out the box.

"I hope you like them," Valerie said, trying to take a peek at the ones he was wearing. They were gold but she couldn't make out the shape.

Richard's face broke into a broad grin. "Silver and Blue," he said "They're lovely. I haven't got any like these," and he bent over to give her a kiss.

Valerie felt herself blush "Will you excuse me, Richard."

"Of course. I'm ready and waiting," he joked.

Valerie stumbled to the Ladies. How long had she got before she had to tell him the truth? He wouldn't expect to book a weekend away in January, would he? Not in this country. Had she told him her birthday was in January? She might have joked that she was a 'silly goat,' at one stage. She couldn't remember.

She splashed her face with cold water and reapplied her lipstick. How soon before she could ask to go home? The dancing had only just begun. One or two of the more elderly couples were leaving. Perhaps she could stay until they started the flashing lights and disco music, if that is what happened.

Richard was coming away from the bar when she returned to the table.

"I've got you a cocktail." he said, "A Sunrise Special- as I'm on the hard stuff."

Valerie thought for a moment that he was kidding. Surely he wasn't going to drink more before he drove her home?

"Don't look so worried," he said," It's almost all ginger ale. Now, about your TV. The thing is, the stall was manned by a woman, if that makes any sense. One of the boys took a photo of the van. It belongs to a chap called Simmons. It was his wife, Barbara, on the stall."

"Eric Simmons?"

"Yes. Do you know him?"

"I was with him last week. He's our relief postman."

"So he would have known you were away?"

"I suppose so."

"Well, I expect they'll have picked him up by

now."

"But I don't want my old TV back."

"Don't worry. It would have taken ages and confused things with the insurers."

"Oh dear, more problems."

"Come on, love, life's not that bad. We've got that weekend to look forward to. You do want to take it, don't you?"

Now's my chance, Valerie thought. I can tell him now, while we are in company. But she was too afraid. After all she had to rely on him to take her home.

"Let's get Christmas over, first," she said. "Keep it for the New Year."

He gave her a hug and kissed the top of her head. She'd made sure he enjoyed the evening. It was the least she could do.

Chapter 16

Monday afternoon Valerie waited on the station platform for the train home. Then, out of the corner of her eye, she noticed a familiar shape. It was the delivery man from the store. He was wearing a grey hoodie but she would recognise him anywhere as he stood at least two inches above the people around him. What was he doing waiting for a train? Was he following her? Surely he had a vehicle of his own? When the train stopped she entered the carriage swiftly and pushed her way through two more until she felt it was safe to sit down. She had to ask a sulky young woman to move her bag in order to take a seat but there was no sign of the delivery man and when she reached her stop she didn't see him alight.

It wasn't until the next morning, when Judy rang her bell before she had even begun her breakfast, that the mystery began to deepen.

"Did you see that man watching your house last night?" said Judy.

"A man? What man? What did he look like?"

"He was big, in a grey hooded top, walking up and down with his hands in his pockets. I didn't like the look of him."

"How long was he there?"

"About twenty minutes. He wasn't waiting for you, was he?"

"I hope not. I think I know who it might be but I don't like the idea that he might be stalking me. If he's who I think it is I will see him today. I could ask him."

"Do you think that's wise?"

"Don't worry. I'll do it in the canteen when there's

plenty of people about. Thanks for looking out for me, Judy."

"As long as you're safe."

"I will be, don't you worry."

Her heart was thumping when she entered the canteen at lunch time, wondering if she would see the man she thought was the driver but there was no sign of him.

She didn't know the rest of the men well enough to ask after him but she did need to know what had happened.

Timidly, she knocked on the office door and asked for the supervisor.

When she asked what had happened about the sofa the woman looked annoyed.

"Thanks to you we had to let him go and not only him, his partner as well. He was the one that confessed to taking the sofa into the country and dumping it. It wasn't a very pleasant interview. Now we have to advertise for two more drivers."

Valerie was concerned. Had the man discovered where she lived and was she in danger?

She tried to remember what he looked like. This was another disadvantage of living alone. She would tell Judy when she got home. She probably didn't have enough evidence to contact the police.

She found herself looking round and hurrying along the road when she left the station that evening. There was nobody in her street and no strange cars that she could see, although the road was so narrow and so many houses had vehicles that she might not have noticed if a space had been taken by a stranger. It was more likely that the occupant of the house would spot them and ask them to move on.

She did not go to her own door straight away. Instead, she rang the bell for Judy's house and was relieved when she answered at once, opening it wide and waving towards the kitchen.

"This is great. I've been meaning to catch up with you. How are things?"

"I've really come about that man you saw. I think he may be stalking me." She told her friend about the sofa and the fact that the driver had been sacked.

"Pete is always on about folk who fly tip. It gives builders like him a bad name," responded Judy. "Have you told the police?"

"Not yet, they'll think I am a silly nuisance. But if we see him again I might. He didn't seem to be doing anything, did he?"

"No, just hanging about. It could have been someone innocent, waiting for a mate. I didn't see him go."

"The trouble is, I'll be afraid to go out in the evenings now, unless someone is with me. I don't want to live like that."

"We'll keep a lookout. It might not happen again. Are you OK tonight?"

"Yes, I feel better now I've told you. Thanks, Judy."

She didn't want to stay, she could see Judy was cooking dinner. She would try to put the man out of her mind. The house was as secure as she could make it and Richard was always on the other end of the phone.

She had just put the key in the lock when a shape emerged from behind the hedge. "You bitch," he growled. "You lost me my job." His hand was raised and she could see the flash of a knife. She tried to scream but it came out as a choked squeak.

"Valerie, you forgot your bag," a voice called from the neighbouring doorway.

The man was distracted, the knife dropped from his hand and he turned away, pushing past Judy as she flung herself at him but couldn't stop him racing down the road.

Valerie collapsed onto her doorstep. "Thanks," she managed to gasp as the door swung open and she fell inside.

"That was the man, wasn't it?" said Judy as she helped Valerie onto a chair. "I think a cup of tea is in order. Did you get a good look at him?"

"I think so – but I also got a smell. It was oil or petrol or something strong and unpleasant. He had stubble. I think I remember him, now."

"You must tell them at work." she said, as the kettle boiled. "I'll ring the police. They'll take notice of two of us and there's the knife."

"Don't touch it!"

"Don't worry, I've seen enough TV crime dramas to know they will want fingerprints. He may even be on their database. Here, I've sugared it," and she handed Valerie a mug of tea.

"They will think I'm a sad case."

"That doesn't matter, as long as you're safe. That's what they're here for."

Chapter 17

As soon as Judy had told the local police they knew exactly who they were dealing with. It wasn't long before they had picked him up and charged him and she felt brave enough to tell Richard about her experiences.

"Relax," he told her. "I'll watch out for you. It won't be for a while. Meanwhile he's locked up – well out of the way. He's someone we have had our eye on for a while and when your neighbour gave us the knife we had plenty to charge him with. You'll be used to giving statements by now. We'll let you know when it comes to court."

"I'm not too popular at work," she said. "It's a good job we have a little break at Christmas."

But Christmas was going to be difficult as Richard expected to see her over the holiday.

"I want you to meet my family," he had suggested. "How about Boxing Day?" but Valerie knew his daughter might sense there was something wrong.

"I"ll have to invent an illness," Valerie told Judy that evening. "I don't want to give his family the impression that we are an item. Can I say your lunch gave me food poisoning?"

"If you must. How long are you going to go on lying to him?"

"Until the New Year. I must tell him then but I'm afraid of how he'll react. He's got a bit of a temper."

"Can't you manufacture a row?"

"How do I do that?"

"Say you've seen him with someone else. He'd understand that."

"But I haven't."

"Get Fiona to send him someone."

"Now, that might work. Thanks, Judy."

Valerie rang Fiona from work and explained her dilemma.

"Richard told me not to send any more people," Fiona said. "He said he'd found the perfect partner."

"Well he was mistaken- and it's probably my fault." Valerie said. "I was enjoying his company, most of the time, although he did make me nervous when he shouted at other drivers. It seemed a bit over the top."

"Some men are like that behind the wheel," Fiona replied. "He's never frightened you, has he? If so we'll have to be careful who we send."

"No- but I don't think he likes to be contradicted."

"How about an actress? I think I know someone who might be willing to help."

"Do you really? I wouldn't want to cause any more upsetment."

"It's fine. She did ask about him and I said he was satisfied. I'm sorry it didn't work out for you, Valerie. We tried."

"I know, but I've probably got enough to keep me busy for now. Thank you, Fiona. If we can pull this off without hurting Richard's feelings too much it will be down to you."

"I can ask him if he wants to meet her, say she really liked his profile. She's very pretty, but I think she's been going out with the wrong type of man."

"I'll try to be unavailable for a while. I was dreading being invited to a New Year Party. I don't like staying up so late."

"But you didn't mind with Connor?"

Valerie blushed. "That taught me a lesson. I

thought I was a better judge,"

"He fooled us all. He was very charming. He never contacted us again. I don't suppose he got in touch with you?"

"No, there was no apology, no explanation, nothing. I'm glad I never invited him into my home. He would have spoilt all my memories and left me reminded of how gullible I had been. I think maybe I'm safer on my own. You know where you are with plants – if you take care of them they flourish and don't let you down"

"Why not give it a rest for six months. You might feel different then."

"If I can extricate myself from Richard without hurting him I'll be content."

To Valerie's surprise and relief she had an email from her sister.

I've been in touch with Mum and she wants us to get together for Christmas.

It had been months since she had visited her parents in Wales. What could have made them want to play happy families now?

Her father had been strong minded and her mother would never disagree with him. Both daughters were eager to escape and make their own lives. Valerie had returned to the caravan park that they both owned after James's death but it had not been a happy reunion. She had a sinking feeling that something must be wrong.

Her premonition proved correct. When she rang her mother to clarify matters the truth came out. Her father was unwell. It was likely this would be his last Christmas and she wanted to make it memorable.

"Christine has promised to come over for a whole

week," she explained. "We have plenty of empty vans. It would be lovely if you could join us."

All Valerie's memories of her time with her parents were tinged with regret. She had tried to love her father but she could never respect him and although she cared for her mother, it made her angry to see how she behaved in his presence, like a meek little mouse.

However, there was something in Florence's voice that made Valerie think that there may have been changes. Had her father's illness changed the balance of power in the household?

The only way to find out was to accept the invitation. It would certainly solve a lot of her present problems.

When Valerie told Richard she was going away for Christmas as her father was ill he went very quiet. She was afraid he was going to lose his temper again but he just shrugged.

"When are you coming back?" he asked.

"I don't know. I'm due back on the second of January but if I'm needed at home I'll stay longer. My sister is coming over from America but I don't expect she'll be able to stay long, either."

"Your new job will be OK?"

"It's too bad if it isn't. It's just a good thing I hadn't moved. There was too much going on, Richard. Getting away might be good for me. I expect Christmas is a busy time for you, too."

"The privileges of rank. I can take more time off now, but I'll have nobody to spend it with."

"I'll be back. There's too much keeping me here for me to be away for too long."

Richard didn't ask for details. He wasn't to know that she meant Bertie and the allotment. In fact, it was

Bertie that was concerning her. It was over five foot high and the pot was now on a tray on the floor as it was too tall for the coffee table. Judy had a spare key for her house. Could she trust her to look after her precious rubber plant? After all, he was more than a mere plant to her. She used him to help her sort out her options, be sensible when she was being indecisive. Without him she would have made even more stupid decisions. She might even have invited one or more of her men friends into her house. Somehow, just having Bertie watching over her kept her sane. After all that had happened he seemed like some sort of talisman, almost a guardian angel.

"Anyone would think I was daft," she told him, "but Judy will look after you until I get back."

Chapter 18

Now all she had to do was ask Joe to keep an eye on her half of the allotment. There wasn't much to do but she didn't want him worrying if she didn't turn up one weekend.

She was glad she hadn't accused him of being part of the burglary. I was an idiot to suspect him of being involved, Valerie thought and vowed to try to make it up to him.

She'd baked a banana cake and took it with her at the weekend before she was due to leave.

Joe was sitting in his hut staring forlornly out of the window.

"What's up, Joe?" Valerie asked.

"Just winter blues, Val." Joe replied.

"I've got something to cheer you up – put the kettle on."

She took the lid off the cake tin and placed the cake on it. "Cake knife?"

"Wow! What kind of cake?"

"It's a banana cake. Is that OK?"

"Wonderful. I love home made cake."

He handed her a knife and poured the tea into two mugs while she cut them each a large slice of cake.

"You never told me what your job is, Joe." Valerie asked.

"I don't usually talk about it."

"Why not? Are you with the Security Services?"

Joe laughed. "Nothing like that. It's just that when I tell people they seem to shy away from me. I'm a dustman."

"A refuse collector?"

"If you want to sound posh. It's the same thing."

"You're not on my round."

"No, I'm in Littlehampton."

"Do you like it?"

"Yes, I do. I like the blokes I work with. I like the hours. I like being outdoors. There's a lot to like."

"Have you always been a dustman?"

"No. When I left University I thought I would be a landscape gardener. I'd studied landscape management and horticulture, but I couldn't get a job. Then I tried estate agency but it was all facts and figures. I wasn't into buildings, I like trees and plants, so I became a free lance gardener but I couldn't make a living. I still do one or two of my old customers' gardens but being a dustman pays the bills. Laurence and I even bought our own house but it's very complicated. He still pays his half of the mortgage but I have all the other expenses."

"How did you two meet?"

"He's a pharmacist. He was in the chemist's when I went in and happened to mention I was looking for property. Neither of us could afford a deposit on our own but we went for a drink and took it from there."

"Oh, Joe, no wonder you look glum. What are you doing for Christmas?"

"I'm helping at the hospital. There's always a lovely atmosphere there. Why do you ask?"

"Because I'll be away. I'm going to Wales. My father is ill and my sister is coming over from the States. It will be the first family Christmas for years."

"I hope it works out all right."

"That's why I asked. I hoped you'd watch over my half of the allotment. Dig up anything that's left, if you like."

"I could break up the earth for potatoes."

"Don't overdo it. Have some time off."

"What about Bertie?"

"Judy's looking after him. He's almost as tall as me, now. Here. Keep the tin. I've more at home," and she replaced the cake.

She was suddenly afraid that he was going to ask about her love life and she hadn't told him about Connor. Thinking about him was too painful. She'd spent night after night tossing and turning, unable to sleep, wondering why she hadn't guessed he was too good to be true. He hadn't been in touch and she didn't have a photograph of him but his image stayed in her memory. Nobody, she thought, would ever capture her heart like that again. She forced herself back to the present and heard Joe ask, "What happened about your move?"

"I told the agent not to send anyone else. I'd only had one couple interested and I can't cope with the idea of it at the moment. I'm waiting until the Spring. I'm not sure I want to live in a flat. I don't seem sure about anything right now."

"Maybe a trip to Wales will clarify things."

"I hope so. It will certainly be a change. My parents run a caravan park."

"A good place for a holiday?"

"Perhaps. Christine and I will have one to stay in while we're there."

"Do you and your sister get on?"

"Most of the time. But we're very different. She's attractive and ambitious."

"And you are?"

"Don't tease. I'm just ordinary."

"No-one could call you ordinary."

"Stop the soft soap. I'm off. See you in the New Year."

"Sure. Happy Christmas, Valerie, and thanks for

the cake."

"You're welcome."

It was a cold , crisp day when Valerie boarded the train for Wales. She liked travelling by rail. Of course it would have been cheaper to go by coach but it took so much longer.

She had a reserved seat from London and wondered if anyone would be seated next to her.

"Here, let me help you with that," a rich masculine voice said in her ear as she lifted her case onto the rack above her seat.

"Thank you," Valerie said, turning her head to look at the stranger.

The man had a thin, bearded face and bright blue eyes. His hair was long and tied back in a ponytail.

Once he had lifted her case he added one of his own – a musical instrument, she guessed.

"You're a musician?" Valerie enquired as they sat down.

"Does it show?" he grinned.

"What do you play?"

"Guess."

"A clarinet?"

"Spot on."

"Are you with a band?"

"More a group than a band. The Verdant Valley Stompers. I don't suppose you've heard of us."

"What kind of music?"

"Well – did you know the Temperance Seven or the Barron Knights?"

"I think so. They were back in the sixties, weren't they?"

"We're like a mixture. We do a mix of folk, jazz and spoof covers, not serious – we aim to amuse."

"You've got a gig?"

"Yes, in the middle of nowhere, somewhere unpronounceable. It's on a holiday camp."

"Not Home Farm?"

"Yes. Why, do you know it?"

"It's my parents' site. I didn't know they'd started putting on entertainment. That's where I'm going."

"Great. My name's Jason, Jason Swann , but I don't – chase swans, that is, and you are?"

"Valerie Davies."

"Have you a middle name?"

"Yes, Olive, but I don't like it. It was Popeye's girlfriend's name and it's too old fashioned."

"I think it's a pretty name."

"How would you like to be called Jason Linseed Swann?"

"Not everyone thinks of Olive Oil when they hear that name but I get what you say. Now you've put the image in my head I'll never get rid of it!"

Valerie giggled and sat back in her seat. She certainly had a fascinating companion – but she hoped he would allow her some time for a snooze. It was a long journey to Wales.

Chapter 19

Home Farm Holiday Park looked rather desolate when Jason and Valerie arrived by taxi from the station. The surrounding trees were bare, the flower beds empty and the sign on the gate needed a coat of paint.

"How many people were you expecting?" Valerie asked.

"Goodness only knows. I didn't do the booking. It just seemed somewhere warm to hide out for a few days."

"Do you need to hide out?"

"Not really. I didn't mean it to sound like that. It's just that we are skint and spending Christmas with all our bed and board thrown in seemed like a good option."

"How long are you here for?"

"Nine days. We cover Christmas and both weekends. Do your family get many visitors in the winter?"

"I don't think so, but there's a number of residential vans. They'd be glad to see you. How are the rest of the group getting here?"

"Vic's got a van. They're coming from Ashford. Don't expect they'll get here until later tonight."

"Well, come on, let's get you introduced, find you a home and discover what Mum has planned."

The reception area was warm and welcoming and Florence, Valerie's mother, was behind the desk.

"Valerie, darling," she exclaimed. "It's lovely to see you – and who is this young man?"

"He's not with me, Mum. He's part of the band."

"The Verdant Valley Stompers? Are you on your own?"

"Yes. The rest are coming by van."

"Well, you've got two mobile homes, pitches seventeen and eighteen. If you wait here a moment I'll see to Valerie first."

"I can wait, Mum."

"No. I must take you to your father. Christine's already here. She'll get you up to speed with everything that's been going on."

Valerie's parents lived in the only other building on the site – a brick bungalow behind the main hall. It was a quiet, sheltered spot, surrounded by tall trees yet with easy access to the beach. Valerie's heart beat faster with trepidation. How sick was her father? Was he in pain? Would he recognise her?

She was pleasantly surprised to see him sitting in his favourite chair by the fire. Christine was seated opposite on a rather ancient sofa.

"Look who's here, Douglas!" said Florence as they entered.

"Val, my sweet." her father held out his arms. "Excuse me for not getting up. This is a real treat – both my daughters home for Christmas."

Valerie hugged him gratefully, aware of Christine stiffening as she did so.

"Sorry I've been away so long," Valerie began and then realised her comment could be interpreted as a dig at Christine.

"It doesn't matter." her father responded. "You're here now. Your mother has been so excited."

"Is there anything you need, Dad?" Christine asked.

"No, not now. After Christmas we'll talk business.

110

For now lets just enjoy being together."

"Right, I'll be with Mum," said Christine, and left the room.

"She doesn't change," Valerie sighed.

"No, but she's a good girl at heart. She's just got an ambitious streak. It makes her less sympathetic. How are you managing, darling?"

"I'm OK. I've been meeting lots of people but nobody as perfect as James. I've got a new job, nearer home and I've still got the allotment."

"You're settled, then?"

Valerie gave a bitter laugh. "I suppose so- until something better comes along, a knight in bright, shiny armour!"

"They must be pretty rare in Sussex."

"Enough about me. How's the caravan business? I see you've added a social area."

"We had to. All the other camps had dance halls and amusement arcades. We had to compete."

"And you've got a band over Christmas?"

"Yes, that brought a lot of new customers. We're almost fully booked."

"But there's room for us?"

"Yes, you and Christine have one of our superior mobile homes."

"That will suit her."

Valerie's mother pushed the door open and put a mug of tea on the coffee table.

"Now, let Valerie get settled in," she said, "I'll bring your dinner in later."

"Right, dear." Valerie watched the caring look that passed between them and felt a flash of envy.

"How is Dad, really?" Christine asked when they joined her in the kitchen.

"He puts a brave face on it but it's not good.

Having you two here will help but he won't be with us next Christmas." Florence stopped, took a deep breath and continued. "He wants to get his affairs in order. He's hoping we will agree with his plans. I told him to leave it until after Christmas."

"What kind of plans?" Christine asked.

"Don't you worry about it," Florence replied. "It will all become clear in a few days time."

But Christine was not easy to convince. When they were on their own she complained to Valerie. "I suppose he means his will, and the camp. Mother couldn't carry on running the place on her own, could she?"

"I think she could – but let's just wait and see, shall we? It'll do no good fretting about it. The band's on tonight. Let's go and listen to them."

"I'm too tired. I don't like modern music. You go. I'll check in with Tyrone. Tomorrow I must remember to take some snaps of the camp. He and Junior would like that."

Junior! thought Valerie, how American, and began to unpack her case and select her outfit for the evening.

There was a massive Christmas tree in the corner of the hall and coloured lights round the walls. The stage was brightly lit with a drum kit and instruments in situ.

Valerie wondered if they were going to introduce themselves or if there was an MC. The room filled up with people sitting at little tables or standing by the bar at the rear of the room.

There was an expectant hum and Valerie had to subdue her disappointment at not being able to share the experience with anyone. She'd chosen a table near the back of the room so it didn't look too obvious that she was alone.

The lights dimmed and a spotlight shone on the stage. On strode a middle aged man with an evening suit and a bow tie. He introduced himself as Mike Mace, the compère for the evening.

"Welcome to Home Farm. Let's hope the only turkeys we have this week are on our dinner plates," he began. A few titters came from the audience,

. I hope he doesn't consider himself a comedian, thought Valerie, and stopped listening.

"Can I buy you a drink?" asked a quiet voice behind her.

"Oh, thank you. I didn't think..." she stuttered.

"I could see you were in the world of dreams," said the man. "You won't remember me. I'm Evan, the gardener."

Valerie looked at his brown weather beaten face and the thick white hair.

"I do remember you. Do you still take care of the site?"

"Yes. It doesn't need much looking after. Sometimes I just pick up litter. What would you like?"

"I'll have a bitter lemon, thank you. Are you staying for the show?"

"Some of it. I like to spot if there are any potential trouble makers."

"So you're the security, too?"

"Yes, general dogsbody. I'll be back in a mo."

By the time Evan returned the announcer was introducing the Verdant Valley Stompers and they began their set. The music was too loud to talk over so the two of them just sat and listened.

Valerie watched the audience. There were quite a

lot of families with children of all ages, even a few with babies in buggies who seemed able to sleep through the whole event.

One or two young children began to run around and dance in front of the stage but nobody made a nuisance of themselves and the few tables with teenage boys and girls seemed happy enough to be together in a crowd. She did wonder if they would pair off later and cause problems but that would be nothing to do with her.

"They don't hire vans to groups of single men or girls, do they?" Valerie asked Evan in the break.

"No, it's not site policy, but there are some families who come every year and the youngsters know each other. That's why they sit together. As they get older it gets harder to keep an eye on them. I just watch out in case anyone brings drugs onto the camp. Booze we can cope with, drugs, we'd have to bring in the law."

By ten o'clock Valerie had had enough and said goodnight to her companion. Christine was already in her bunk, reading a novel and Valerie got ready for her bed as quietly as she could, not wanting to disturb her. She knew her sister was not one for conversation and she was happy to slide under the duvet and go to sleep.

Chapter 20

Valerie was woken by a shrill scream and shouts coming from the direction of the Community Hall.

Climbing out of bed she went to the window but the lighting at the camp was quite dim and only at junctions. There did seem to be movement in the distance.

"What is it?" Christine asked, appearing at her elbow.

"Some sort of commotion. It sounds like a fight," Valerie replied. "I think I'll take a look."

"Hang on, I'll come with you," and the two sisters quickly donned coats and shoes and set off towards the noise.

Sure enough a group of people were crowded round a body on the ground. He wasn't dead, but blood was pouring from his nose and he was holding his arm as if it was injured.

Valerie recognised him. It was Jason, from the band, and two of his friends were trying to get him to stand up.

"Leave him," Christine commanded. "What's happened here?"

"This twerp tried to chat up Max's girlfriend," a young man informed them. "Max got angry and socked him."

"Where's Max now?"

"Pushed off. She told him to get lost."

"And where's the girl?"

"She went, too."

"So they might be together?"

"I hope not," said another girl. "He's not in a very good mood."

"Is she in danger?" Valerie asked and the youngsters looked at each other and said nothing.

Jason staggered to his feet, hugging his arm.

"We'll look after him," a band member said. "You'd better find the others."

"How do you feel, Jason?" Valerie asked.

"Not too bad, sorry about this."

"You take care. What's her name?"

"Miriam."

"Which vans were they in?" Christine asked.

"Numbers four and five," was the response.

"OK. We'll check them first. I guess their parents are in there."

"Two of them are," came a voice from the darkness. "We're Miriam's parents. We heard a noise. She's not with us and she left her phone on the bed." He waved a torch round the group as if he might find her among the onlookers.

"Right, we'll check Max's place first then spread out. They can't have gone far."

"Shouldn't we call the police?" asked Miriam's mother.

"If we don't find them in the next half hour, yes," Christine responded, "but let's hope it isn't necessary. Mrs ?"

"Brown, " answered her husband.

"Right. Mr Brown, If you take a couple of Miriam's friends down to the beach, Valerie and I will take groups down the road, both ways. When you've settled Jason perhaps the rest of you could cover the camp. Back here in 30 minutes and we'll decide what to do next."

"Do you think they're together?" Valerie asked.

"It will be easier if they are. If we find one and not the other it won't be a good sign."

After waking Max's parents and being joined by Evan the two groups separated and started off along the road, calling for the lost pair.

They'd hardly left the entrance to the camp when there was a shout from the woods. Mr Brown was pulling a young man behind him as he stepped into the light.

"We've found the little runt," he growled, "but he won't tell us where Miriam is."

"I haven't seen her," wailed the boy. "I don't know where she is. Let go of me." He looked around for support but none seemed forthcoming.

"Did she follow you?" Christine asked.

"Yes. She tried to tell me it was nothing. She was flattered. I didn't want to listen. I said I'd had enough. I couldn't trust her. I was going up the hill to cool off. Then I couldn't see the path. I've been stuck in that blessed wood for ages."

"Why didn't you ring for help?"

"I couldn't. My phone needs charging. Besides, I was too wound up."

"When she left you, which way did she go?"

"Towards the beach, I think, not back to the camp."

"OK, folks," said Evan, taking charge. "Let's try the beach. Mr Brown, you go first. Once we get out in the open we'll be able to see without the torches."

He was right, once they were beyond the trees the moonlight was glistening on the water. It seemed such a peaceful scene.

"Let's split into two groups," said Evan. "Mr Brown, your group go that way and your wife, Valerie, Christine and I will go the other way. Look out for any places someone might hide."

I hope she didn't go into the water, Valerie thought, but did not dare voice her fears.

A few hundred yards along the beach they came to a small jetty. The water lapped gently at the wooden supports.

"Was there a boat here?" Christine asked.

"Yes," Evan responded. "It's gone. I tied it up securely. Someone's moved it. It's only a rowing boat."

"Where would she row to?" Christine asked. "There's no island."

"She'd be taken by the current. As long as it is coming in it flows this way," Evan replied, running along the beach. The sand was giving way to rocks and they were heading for cliffs. Soon they would have to leave the water's edge.

"Should we call the coastguard?" Valerie asked.

"No look!" Christine pointed to a rocky outcrop. "There's the boat!"

"Miriam, Miriam," shouted her mother, racing along the sand. As they followed her a bedraggled young woman stepped out of a cave. Valerie could see she had been crying. Her face was red and blotchy and she was shivering with cold.

"Come here, my love," said Mrs Brown, taking off her coat and wrapping it round her daughter's shoulders. "What were you thinking of?"

"I hate him," cried the girl. "I just wanted to get away and think. I'm sorry, Mum. I would have come back. I'm sorry."

"Shh. It's all right now we've found you. None of it matters. Let's go back and tell your father you're safe. He was so worried."

"It was Max. I thought he was going to follow me.

I didn't know what he would do."

They all began walking back to the camp, Mrs Brown comforting the the shivering girl as best she could.

"I'll just pull the boat up a bit higher," Evan said. "I'll bring it back in the morning."

Christine ran ahead to catch up with the other group and they all returned to the hall.

"Where's Jason?" Miriam asked.

"He's back in his own van," was the reply, "and Max has gone home, too. You're quite safe."

"I think he'd been drinking, not just from the bar. He had something with him. He's not always like that."

"How well do you know him?"

"Not very well at all. We were together all last summer but we've only been messaging since then. I think he was hoping for too much, but I'm only seventeen. I'm not ready for a serious relationship."

"He's been texting about you for weeks," said one of his friends. "It was just showing off."

"I didn't know. I'm so sorry," and she burst into tears again.

"Come on let's get you to bed," said Mr Brown. "We can sort it all out in the morning."

The group dispersed and Christine and Valerie began to make their way to their van.

"We don't have to worry Mum, do we?" Valerie asked.

"Not if she didn't hear anything," Christine replied, but they were unlucky. There were lights on in the bungalow. "I expect Evan would tell her, anyway," said Valerie. "We'd better let her know it's all sorted."

Florence was waiting in the hallway for them and opened the door as soon as they came up the path.

"What on earth's going on?" she demanded.

"There's been a fracas," Valerie said, "but it's over now. One of the boys got jealous when a band member took an interest in his girlfriend. They're all back in their vans now."

"Was anyone hurt?"

"I think Jason got a bloody nose but otherwise everyone's OK, just cold."

"Oh dear, I never thought. You must be freezing. Come in and I'll make a hot drink."

"Thanks, Mum," Christine said, and Valerie realised her sister looked exhausted.

"I told Donald that having a band might be too much," Florence said when they were seated round the kitchen table with mugs of hot chocolate.

"You never know with strangers. It would be much easier if everyone knew each other."

"Would you have to change things round -if you didn't have any holiday vans?" Valerie asked.

"I think the plots would have to be bigger. The residential vans have little gardens and we'd probably have to change the parking arrangements. It's too much to consider now."

"I wonder if the band will stay for the rest of the holiday?" Valerie mused.

"They've signed a contract," Florence replied. "Maybe Jason will be well enough to sing."

"As long as Evan can keep the peace."

"He's getting on. Perhaps we ought to hire a younger security man. You know he's playing Santa for the little ones tomorrow?"

"He'll be great. But it's tomorrow already. We'd better get back. Thanks, Mum. Happy Christmas."

Chapter 21

It was a bleary eyed Valerie who rose the next morning and urged her sister to get out of bed.

"We said we'd be there for breakfast at nine. Donald will be expecting us," she urged.

It had not been easy to think of presents to take for everyone but Valerie had brought some jars of home-made jam for her parents and a leather bound diary for Christine.

She received a new pair of gardening gloves from Donald and Florence and a book entitled "The Beauties of America," from Christine, which turned out to be full of photographs of landscapes and parks.

"This is lovely," Valerie exclaimed. "Thank you, Christine."

"Thought you'd like it," Christine responded. "We've been to some of those places. Junior is into Geology."

"You must be very proud," said Florence.

"It might be just a phase - but he's doing OK at school."

"And Tyrone?"

"He's into fishing. When he's not at work he's away with the boys. I don't see him much."

"But you're glad you moved there?"

"Yep. It's a good life and I get to do the odd advert. Pity you don't get them over here."

Valerie said nothing. Having a sister who was a model had been difficult while Christine was in England but she had forgotten she would probably continue when she was abroad. Of course she was too old for the kind of glamour modelling she used to do before her marriage but it was easy to imagine her doing adverts for working mothers or holidays. She didn't ask.

After Christmas lunch they listened to the Queen's speech and then went their separate ways. Douglas went to sleep. Florence dozed in front of the TV. Christine went back to the van and Valerie decided to go for a walk. She would make her way down to the beach. It was a cold, dry, day with a light breeze and being with so many people had made her long for a little peace and quiet.

Maybe I do need to be on my own, she thought. Perhaps looking for a partner is the wrong thing to do. Yet there must be more to life than work and solitude. She thought of Joe, helping out in a hospital to stop himself feeling lonely over Christmas. If only I could be that unselfish, but I don't seem to have the inner strength to keep giving. Is it too much to ask that I find someone to help me get through life – like Mum and Dad have always had each other?

Thinking of her father made her remember what her mother had said about Christmas. She must have been told his illness was terminal. How long did he have? He must be wanting to arrange everything for the future and having Christine and her together was part of that planning. Of course, he must be going to tell them what was in his will. He didn't want any arguments after he had gone. He was thinking about Florence, just as she had always considered him.

Valerie stood and looked at the ocean. We don't live very long, when you think of it. We really need to make the most of every moment. I will keep looking for another partner. I want to be able to leave something, someone, behind but I'll be super careful who I get involved with from now on.

Donald had, indeed, gathered them together to tell them his plans for the future.

"Of course I'm leaving everything to Florence," he said, "but I need reassurance that you girls will do your best to help out. Flo will have to decide when it becomes too much for her and you must promise me you'll be ready to advise her if she has to sell."

"It won't come to that," Florence interrupted.

"You won't be able to carry on for ever, my love," Donald said. "It's been hard enough for us both to keep it going these last few years."

"But people are returning to staycations, aren't they?" Valerie asked. "What with Global warming and Europe getting more expensive."

"We did have a good year this year," Florence remarked, "and bookings are up for next year. We get a lot of families who come back time and again."

"It might be just a phase," Christine said. "You can't guarantee the weather, especially in Wales."

"It's a lovely spot," Valerie said. "If I had a family I'd like to come here."

"There's a new children's playground," Donald said proudly, "and an exercise area for dogs, but the nature trail needs updating. It's too much work for Evan and we can't afford to hire anyone else."

"How much do you make in a year?" Christine asked.

Florence and Donald looked at each other.

"We have an accountant," Florence began.

"You mean, you don't know?"

"We have enough to live on."

"I have an assessment at the bank every April," Donald said. "We're in profit."

"And if you get a big expense – can you cope?"

"We haven't bought any new vans. The one you are

in was our last purchase and we are insured for accidents. We know what we're doing, love."

"Then you don't need us to supervise you, do you?" said Christine. "I can't keep coming back to check on things."

"Oh, Chrissie, don't be such a grump," said Valerie. "There's no need to worry, Dad. I'm willing to help Mum. In fact I'm thinking of moving. If it gets too much for her I'll up sticks and come over."

"Thank you, love," Florence said. "But that won't be necessary for a while. Now, let's stop being miserable and have tea. We can start the Christmas cake."

Donald lay back on his pillows.

I hope he's satisfied, thought Valerie. He doesn't need any extra stress at this time.

Christine was first out of the room.

"I didn't come here for this," she snapped. "I wanted to invite you all over to the States for Junior's graduation. Mum, I think you should have retired years ago. It's obviously too much for you both."

"Don't take on so, Chrissie," Florence said. "I'm sorry it's such a shock. I should have prepared you but there's nothing you, or the doctors can do, except keep him pain free if possible and don't blame the camp. If we hadn't had that to keep us busy we'd have shuffled off our mortal coil years ago."

"He does seem very calm about it," Valerie said.

"That's the best way to be. Now, you two girls be sensible. Do whatever he asks. Keep things peaceful."

Valerie could see Christine was trying not to cry, whether with pity or frustration, she didn't know.

"We're here to make him feel things are OK," she said to her sister. "Put on a brave face. Everything will work out in the end."

Valerie lay on her bed that night, looking at the ceiling.

Christine had tried, half heartedly, to get Florence to agree to selling the site and moving to America but their mother refused to entertain the idea.

"I'm sad that I haven't seen my grandson grow up but what would I want to be doing living in another country at my time of life?" she said. "I want to end my days here -even if I no longer own the site."

"How much do you think it is worth?" Christine asked Valerie when they were alone together.

"As a going concern or a piece of land?" Valerie replied. "I couldn't say – but it's not come to that yet. Dad might go on for months. Just take each day as it comes."

"But I'm only here for the rest of the week."

"Then leave things to me. We'll keep you informed. Don't worry. You won't be left out of the decision making."

Her words seemed to calm Christine but Valerie's mind was whirling. Had the failure to sell her home been an omen? Was she destined to carry on when her father died? Should she move to Wales and stay with her mother? Is this what her life would be from now on, running a caravan site?

She had the financial skills and she could see what needed doing to improve things but she didn't want to give up the life she had in England.

Once again she wished James was with her to help her decide. I'm still thinking of James, she said to herself, not Richard, not anyone else. Perhaps there's someone here in Wales for me. Perhaps when I get home things will seem clearer.

Back in Sussex she vowed to do some research into

the holiday business, just in case she was needed in Wales. It did seem rather precarious so she turned her mind to the residential aspect of her parents' site. She needed to know the number of mobile homes the area could accommodate, the ground rent, maintenance costs and all the relevant regulations.

There was a site very close to the allotments and she vowed to herself she would visit the owner and pick their brains, but it turned out it was owned by a large conglomerate which had sites all over the British Isles. She couldn't offer it to them. Her mother would hate that. They'd probably keep her on as manager but she'd have no say in how it was run.

Having a mix of residential mobile homes and holiday pitches had seemed ideal but the mix of age groups could lead to conflict.

Although some of the elderly residents appreciated the extra entertainment and amusements others would have preferred it to remain a quiet oasis with just the shop and a community hall that had occasional speakers and bingo.

Valerie presumed the licence would have to change if it was completely residential but there would be no change of owner as her mother and father had been jointly in charge.

She sat in the kichen and wrote a long letter to David, outlining what she was hoping to do and asking for his advice. Even though she had only been with him for a few hours she felt that with his love of nature and his artistic talent he would be able to help her.

He had already contacted her with photographs of the countryside in his local area and his reply was swift.

"If you would like me to come and illustrate a

brochure for you, I'd be happy to help. I fancy a trip to Wales. Do tell me more about Home Farm. Has it got a website? If not I'd be happy to design one."

Valerie couldn't think of anyone she would rather have to advertise the site. "I'll let you know when I've decided what to do. I haven't told mother what I am planning yet although I'm sure she'll agree."

Her driving lessons were going well and she was enjoying sprucing up the house. She wanted it to look good if there was the chance she would be trying to sell it, again.

Valerie bought some peach paint and redecorated the lounge. Then the kitchen looked tired so she painted the walls white and the woodwork blue. "Who needs white doors everywhere?" she said to Bertie as she watered him "It's a good job you're on the floor now – you're nearly as tall as me."

It was amazing what comfort she got out of having him there to talk to, even if he couldn't respond.

It was also encouraging to find that the instructor she had chosen for her driving lessons was not only patient and efficient but also friendly and communicative.

"Did your husband drive?" Coral asked when Valerie had just mastered a three point turn and they were parked in a quiet street to have a break.

"He could drive," Valerie replied, "but we didn't have a car. He rode a motor bike."

"What was his job?"

"He worked for Trading Standards. He was in West London when we met but after we married we moved here."

"So that's why you worked in London."

"It seemed sensible, at least until we had a family."

"But it never happened?"

"No, and I expect it's too late now."

"Don't give up. You have a lot going for you. Now, mirror, signal, manoeuvre."

Valerie set off again. She'd only had four lessons and she was already beginning to enjoy the sensation of being in charge. For the first two lessons she had thought the car was running away with her and was hesitant about going into fourth gear but Coral had limited their lessons to quiet side roads with few parked vehicles and had praised the efficient way she took to steering. "You'd be surprised how many people don't know their right from their left," she had told Valerie. "You seem to be able to judge distances well. That is going to be a help."

"Do you think I should be looking for a car of my own?" Valerie asked.

"Not unless you have someone to sit with you while you practice. I should wait until you've passed. Of course you could look at some to see which model you would like."

"I think I will. I'd like a hatchback, but it must have a reasonable engine as I could be going backwards and forwards to Wales and there's plenty of hills over there."

"Don't be like one of my other customers who found the ideal car and then didn't buy it because it wasn't in the colour she wanted."

Valerie laughed. She remembered what she had said to Richard about black. In fact she had a secret yearning for one in white but she didn't tell Coral.

Chapter 22

"Now what do I do about my birthday?" she said out loud to Bertie when she got home. She didn't know her colleagues at Chichester well enough to invite them to celebrate with her. In fact there was no-one locally who knew the date. She had always thought it was too near Christmas.

Cards began to arrive and, to her surprise, one from Richard. Of course, anyone who used Ocean Introductions knew her birthday as it was in the details they had been given. She rang to thank him.

"I don't suppose you'd be free for dinner?" Richard asked.

"Oh, Richard. I don't deserve it. I've been so unfair to you."

"No, you haven't. You kept me sane. You helped me through a bad period. I miss you, Valerie. I miss your friendship. Come on, just for old times' sake."

"You make me feel ancient," Valerie laughed. "Where did you have in mind?"

"There's some great restaurants here in Horsham. How about I pick you up at six thirty tomorrow? It will be a change of scene for you."

"Can you make it seven, Richard? It's a work day."

"Maybe you'd prefer the weekend?"

"No, Thursday will be fine. You won't be in uniform, will you?"

Richard laughed. "No, I'll be in disguise. I'll see you, then." and he rang off.

Valerie chose a royal blue midi dress with a blue, red and gold stole for their birthday date.

She had a scarlet handbag to match her red shoes

and she'd popped out in her lunch hour and had her hair styled.

"I'm not bad for 39," she told herself as she looked in the mirror, very aware that the dreaded forty was on the horizon. "I mustn't let my age rule my life. They say you're as old as you feel and I feel good."

Valerie felt even better when she saw how Richard looked at her with admiration when they met.

"You're a sight for sore eyes," he exclaimed. "I forgot how beautiful you are. It's such a pity you won't come on the weekend with me."

"Stop it," Valerie replied. "Don't make me blush. I just want to get things straight. I should apologise for letting Fiona tell you that I didn't think matchmaking had worked in our case."

"That's not quite how she put it. She said she thought I ought to look at some other potential partners as at present you only needed a friend."

"Then she was most diplomatic. It's a hard job, introducing people. She must be constantly worried about whether they are making the right choice."

"It's not her responsibility if they don't get on but I'm glad she introduced us, aren't you? You're so easy to be with."

"Thanks, Richard. I like being with you, too," Valerie replied, but the use of the word 'easy' made the image of Connor's laughing face flash into her mind. It must have shown on her face because Richard asked, "Are you OK, Valerie?"

"Yes, it's nothing. Did you find out any more about the person who attacked me?"

"Bad news, I'm afraid. There were no fingerprints on the knife, you weren't hurt and there was no CCTV in your street. There just wasn't enough evidence to convict him. Of course, he'll be fined for the flytipping and we'll make sure he knows we are watching him, but there's not much else we can do."

"I'll try to put it behind me. Where are we going, Richard?"

The car was turning into the car park of a sports centre.

"It's a surprise. This is where I come to play golf – and it has a very well regarded restaurant."

"That's a relief. I thought for a moment you'd invited me swimming. I wouldn't have thought golf was your thing."

"Too slow? It's a good way of getting to know the movers and shakers in the area. They say women gossip but you should hear what goes at the nineteenth hole."

When they entered the restaurant Valerie understood what he meant. It was almost like stepping into the past with crystal chandeliers, brocade curtains, tied back, white tablecloths and ornate chairs with maroon padded seats.

"It feels kind of historic," Valerie whispered.

"That's because it's an old mansion. The sporting bit is in a modern wing, completely different. This is like being on a cruise ship without the sea sickness, isn't it?"

Valerie giggled. "And is the food just as old fashioned?"

"Well it's not that modern stuff with a prawn and a pea in the centre of the plate and a drizzle of sauce round the edge. Here, take a look at the menu."

At least it's not in French, Valerie thought, wondering if she dare choose a steak. The mushroom soup looked tempting but then she might not have room for a dessert.

"The soup, pork escalopes and lemon mousse, please, Richard."

"You do make up your mind quickly," Richard replied. "I'll have the same, but with jam sponge and custard. I happen to know it is delicious."

"So you've brought someone here before?"

"No-one as lovely as you. I had to try it out, didn't I? Actually I was invited here myself by some new acquaintances."

"You met on the golf course?"

"Yes, and in town. Some of them are local shopkeepers."

"And estate agents?"

"One, why? What has happened about your house sale?"

"It's all stalled, but I may have other plans. I may have to move away."

Their conversation was interrupted by the waiter who took their order and suggested a red wine to go with the meal.

"I'll try it," Richard said, "but if the lady doesn't like it we'll have something else."

Valerie smiled. "I'm not used to different wines," she said, "most of the reds I have tried have been a bit sharp."

"This won't be. I can't drink a whole bottle on my own-especially when I'm driving, but they'll let us take away any we don't drink. Times have changed,"

"You have to be careful now you're an inspector."

"Yes, I wouldn't want to get stopped by one of my own constables. I always finish with coffee. You don't have to worry about my driving."

"I'm in your hands," and she sat back to let the waiter place a bowl of soup on the table in front of her.

"By the way, the Brighton team have arrested your burglar," Richard stated.

"At last. Was he on his own?"

"No-there were three of them – Simmons and two out of work scumbags from London."

"Simmons the scumbag," she joked, glad that she had been able to stop suspecting Joe.

"You light up when you laugh," Richard remarked.

"It's being in good company."

"Here, try the wine."

"Richard? It tastes really great."

"I thought you might like it. We'll keep the bottle. Happy Birthday, Valerie."

He did kiss her when she left the car that evening and she responded. He had made her feel special and she was grateful- but he didn't ask to come in and she was content to give him a cheerful wave as he drove away.

If it wasn't for her father's illness she would be feeling quite satisfied with her life, she thought. She was beginning to make more friends at work. She'd even been with some of them to the theatre.

At first she had been concerned that she had nothing to wear for such an occasion but then she remembered her long Indian cotton skirt and teamed it with a tan, scooped necked, top and a necklace of wooden beads. James had called it her 'ethnic look' and she always felt comfortable in it.

She remembered the awkward feeling she had when she saw the other women, some having dressed up in long skirts and glittering tops and others in casual wear, one even in white leggings and realised that it wasn't the play that had made them meet up for the evening, it was the chance to chatter away like starlings and swap stories of their children. She was about the same age as them but their lives were completely different.

Would she ever experience the pressures and joys of motherhood or was she destined to remain single?

She let herself into the house and switched on the hall light.

Then she held onto the banister as she climbed the stairs, wishing she had taken off her shoes in the kitchen. As she hesitated she felt the rail wobble and come away from the wall. All her weight was on one leg as she was sent flying backwards, hitting her arm on the opposite wall and her head as she landed at the bottom of the stairs. A pain shot up her leg and into her back. She cried out and then everything went black.

She woke in a crumpled heap at the foot of the stairs, unable to move. Her first thought was, I must be paralysed- but she forced herself to wiggle her toes on one foot and found they could still move. The pain in her back was making her breathless. She tried to call out but it was only a feeble squeak.

Think, woman, she told herself. You need to phone someone. She could still turn her head and she looked round for her handbag but it had rolled along the corridor and the contents were scattered across the entrance to the kitchen.

She felt a wave of nausea and fought to keep in control. The nearest telephone was on the hall table but it was up a height. She knew she could never reach it with the injuries to her back and leg. There was one action she could take. She'd seen it in a film and she didn't know if it would work. She might even smash the phone, but it seemed her only hope.

She would have to knock over the table so that the phone dropped onto the floor where she could reach it. Maybe, thought Valerie, I could pull the cord and catch the phone as it falls.

She tried moving into a better position and cried out in agony. Sobbing, she tried to control herself, peering up through her tears at the table. Then she reached out for the wire connecting the phone to the wall and yanked it, hard.

The phone came flying over her head and landed on the bottom step with a sickening crunch, bits of plastic scattering around her. She reached for the receiver but there was no sound. It was completely broken.

"Help." she cried weakly, "Help," and then sank into a stupor.

When she came round some time later it occurred to her that her house was connected to Judy's. If she could knock hard enough on the wall Judy might hear her. I'll do SOS she thought. I don't know if it's three dots and three dashes or three dashes then three dots but if I alternate them it won't matter.

Picking up the remains of the broken phone she hit the wall beside her three times, quickly, and then three times with longer spaces between. She continued until her wrist began to ache. She was feeling very thirsty and her leg was throbbing.

I hope she hears before I faint again, she thought, changing hands. Of course, they'll be upstairs in bed. I should wait until morning. Yet maybe it was morning? She hadn't been wearing a watch and the light in the hall was no longer from the ceiling, but from the little window above the front door. Now she could hear traffic in the street. Judy would be getting up, making breakfast and seeing her husband off to work.

She redoubled her efforts, banging the wall with her fist. "Help me," she shouted. "Help me."

There was a ring on the doorbell and Judy's voice

came through the letterbox.

"Valerie? Was that you banging? Are you all right?"

"Oh, Judy, thank goodness. No, I'm not all right. I've hurt my back and I think my leg's broken. Can you call for an ambulance. I broke the phone."

"Of course. Hang on, I'll get your key. How long have you been there?"

"Since last night. Thanks, Judy. I can't move."

Her shoulders slumped as she heard Judy run back home. It seemed an age before she came back with the key and let herself in.

"I've called an ambulance." she said. "I told them you were concussed. They always think it's more urgent than broken limbs."

Valerie gave a weak smile. "I wish I could go to the loo," she said. "I think I'm going to wet myself."

"If that's all you have to worry about you've been lucky," Judy remarked.

The ambulance drew up outside the house and Judy went out to meet the crew.

"You'll need a stretcher," she said. "She can't move."

"OK, leave it to us," said the paramedic and went inside.

Chapter 23

Valerie didn't remember much for the next few hours. She must have been given a painkiller. It was evening by the time she woke up in hospital, her head fuzzy and her leg in plaster.

"Nurse." she called "Where am I ?"

"You're in Ward Seven," the nurse replied. "You'll be fine. Your spine is bruised but the only thing that was broken was your leg."

"I'm sorry. I must have been a mess."

"Not really. Your neighbour came with you and she's gone back to get some of your own nightclothes. You'll be in bed for a few days. Would you like anything? Water? A sandwich? You missed tea but hot drinks will come round later."

"I don't suppose you've got any chocolate spread?"

The nurse laughed. "I'm not sure that's on the menu."

"A drink of water would be fine, and a digestive biscuit if that's allowed."

"I'm sure it is. If I can find one with chocolate on I'll bring that."

The nurse bustled away and Valerie looked round the ward. Two of the cubicles had their curtains closed but the one opposite her was occupied by an elderly lady who looked very interested in Valerie's predicament.

"Hallo, dear," she began, "I'm Susan. I saw them bring you in."

"Was I shouting?" Valerie asked.

"No. You were so quiet I was worried about you – but you did moan a little before you woke up. What happened?"

"I was an idiot. I fell down the stairs. What happened to you?"

"I got knocked off my scooter. I've only got bruised ribs. I'm going home tomorrow."

Their conversation was interrupted by the arrival of the doctor, accompanied by two nurses. He went to Susan's bed first and Valerie was glad of the time to compose herself.

He looks very attractive, she thought. Rather like David Beckham without the tattoos, and then felt herself blush as he came towards her bed.

"Mrs Davies, I see you are well awake," the doctor said, soothingly. "I'm Dr. Chambers.

How are you feeling?"

"I'm OK, doctor." Her voice came out in a squeak. "How long will I be like this?"

"You'll be with us for a few more days yet. I understand there is no-one at home to help you."

"No."

"Then you must stay until you can manage without support. Are you in pain?"

"Not much, thank you, doctor."

"Well, let nurse know if there's anything you need."

"I will." She sounded so meek to herself. What was it about him that made her heart race and her body tingle? His voice, she thought. He had a smooth, deep voice – and his eyes, they were brown, like his hair which was thick, with a slight curl which gave him an old fashioned 'prince charming' look.

He's bound to be married, Valerie told herself, or, at least, in a relationship. Nobody as gorgeous as that could be a free agent. I wish I didn't look such a sight.

Once the doctor had left she sat back on the pillow.

She hadn't told the truth about the pain. For a second he had made her forget how much her leg and back ached. Her head felt heavy and she was very thirsty. She closed her eyes, trying to remember the accident, wondering if anyone had told Richard, or the shop. Tears came to her eyes. Was there anyone who cared what happened to her?

She must have dozed because the next thing she knew someone was offering her the choice of hot drinks. A jug of water and a tumbler had appeared on her bedside table and a couple of biscuits, not digestives, rich tea.

Valerie tried to hoist herself up into a sitting position.

"Oh, thank you. I'd like cocoa, please, but I must have some water first."

The assistant poured out some water and she drank it eagerly.

She chewed at a biscuit and tasted the cocoa. She felt very alone, unloved and miserable. Her life seemed pointless. She was no use to anyone and nobody would really miss her if she didn't exist. Her cocoa was cold and made her feel sick. All she could do was curl up in the bed and cry.

She must have dozed because the next thing she knew a nurse was standing by her bed.

"I'm off until the morning. Can I get you anything else?" she asked.

"Am I allowed a pain killer?" Valerie asked.

"Yes, if you're not allergic. I'll check your notes."

You won't find much there, Valerie thought. I haven't been able to tell them anything yet, but she accepted what was given to her gratefully, even though the ache she felt was in her mind as much as her body.

Next morning there was a rush and bustle as a new patient was introduced to the ward and Susan went home.

Dr Chambers returned and asked her for more details about her circumstances.

She tried to concentrate but once he had gone she couldn't remember what she had told him.

At least I'm in good hands, she told herself.

Valerie's only other event of any interest was selecting the meals for the following day.

"You'll have whatever you are given today," said the nurse, "as you didn't get the chance to choose yesterday."

Lunch turned out to be a not unacceptable vegetable soup and a ham sandwich, with yogurt to follow. In the afternoon Valerie was given instructions on how to manage some crutches.

By four o'clock she was feeling much more positive about life and was overjoyed to see Judy arrive with a change of clothes and some cosmetics.

"I've got a couple of your own nighties," Judy said. "I didn't bring pyjamas, although I know you have some really nice ones."

"Have you got a hairbrush and comb?" Valerie asked.

"Yes, and a bit of make-up, if it's allowed."

"Probably not – but I'll need underwear for when I come out."

"When will that be?"

"In a couple of days. They're not sure. They're worried about me coping on my own."

"I can help. I'd be glad to."

"But you've got your own family."

"They can manage. As long as I feed them they're happy. I'd rather be with you all day than on my own."

"It wouldn't be all day, but I'll tell the doctor."

"What's he like?"

"Dr Chambers? He's gorgeous. He sat with me for ages just listening while I told him all about myself. I didn't know they had time for that."

"What did you tell him?"

"Only my medical history, my family, my situation, but it was so easy."

"So he had a good bedside manner?" Judy laughed.

"I suppose so. For a time it felt like I really mattered."

"Of course you do, you silly thing. You've your whole life ahead of you. Still, I must run. The others will be wanting their tea. Give me a bell when you're coming out and I'll get Pete to pick you up."

"Oh, Judy, that's so good of you. Thanks."

Chapter 24

It was after a meal of fish pie and jam sponge that Valerie was aware of a trolley being pushed into the ward. Instead of bringing food this trolley had books and magazines and the person pushing it was familiar.

"Joe!" Valerie exclaimed. "What are you doing here?"

"I could ask the same of you," Joe replied. "You know I help out here."

"I thought you only volunteered at Christmas."

"No. I'm here two or three times a week, with the hospital library. Do you want anything to read?"

"What have you got?"

"Romances, thrillers, women's mags, mostly out of date. No gardening magazines, I'm afraid."

"That isn't the only thing I think about."

"How about a travel mag- plan a holiday. Anyway, what happened to you?"

"I fell downstairs, don't laugh."

"Some people will do anything to get attention."

"Joe! You know I'm not like that."

Joe grinned. "Well, if I can't interest you in my books I'll carry on."

"Wait. Give me a couple of novels. I could do with reading about someone else's problems instead of thinking of my own."

"You won't be at the allotment at the weekend, then?"

"No-but there's not a lot to do, is there?"

"Not really. Here, take these. I'll be seeing you."

Valerie felt cheered after seeing him. She'd ask Judy for some paper and a pen. She felt like planning for the Summer, not only the allotment, the rest of her life.

When Judy returned the next day she had three letters with her. Two were bills but the third was from Wales. It was her mother's writing and Valerie felt a shiver of trepidation as she opened it.

"Dear Valerie," it began. "We have been trying to call you without success. I'm sorry to tell you Donald passed away on Sunday. The funeral is Friday week. 11 am at the Crematorium. I hope there is nothing wrong and you have just been out or your battery needs charging. Please call when you get this note. Mum."

"Oh, dear, now what am I going to do?" Valerie cried out. "Just over a week and I'm only just hopping about."

"Bad news?" Judy asked.

"My father's died. I've got to get to Wales."

"I'm so sorry, Valerie. When's the funeral?"

"Friday week. This is a disaster."

"You'll be up and about then, surely?"

"I'll ask the nurse. I can't not go."

When Valerie told the nurse about the letter she was very reassuring. "Dr Chambers said we could discharge you at the weekend," she said. "You'll have plenty of time to get fit to travel."

By Friday afternoon Valerie had called her mother and explained her predicament. "I left my phone at home," Valerie explained. "There was no point worrying you. I'm coming out on Tuesday and a neighbour is helping me. I'll probably travel over next Thursday. I'll let you know when I've made more arrangements." But the idea of making the trip on her own was daunting.

"I'm not sure how strong my leg will be," she told Joe when he came round with the book trolley that afternoon. "I'm going to be in the plaster for weeks."

"How about I take you to Wales?" Joe said.

"You'd have to get time off work."

"They'd give me that as long as I gave them notice. I never take a holiday. I'm not back in until Tuesday afternoon. What time are you coming out?"

"I've no idea. Pete's busy so I'll get a taxi. Judy is going to be waiting for me at home."

"Right. Stay here and have lunch in the restaurant. I'll whizz round and pick you up at three o'clock, if that's not too late."

"It's too much, Joe."

"Nonsense. It's the obvious solution -and don't worry about people getting the wrong impression, Laurence just asked me to join him in France and I'm seriously considering it."

"You are?" Valerie could hardly believe him. "What would you do over there?"

"Laurence wants us to run a vineyard."

"Does he know anything about it?"

"I don't think so. It could be just a passing fancy, but I am rather stuck in a rut."

"That sounds like me. Let's hope we can cheer each other up on the way to Wales. You'll make a horrible journey a lot nicer, thanks, Joe."

Valerie tried to smile but inside she was upset. Once again fate had taught her that nothing stays the same and she would soon have to adjust to another loss in her life.

When the physiotherapist arrived to give her advice about how to carry on out of hospital she was sullen and uncommunicative. So much so that the doctor asked her about it the next day.

"I hear you are having mood swings," he said, diplomatically.

"You could say that. My whole life is crumbling and I haven't the strength or the will to carry on. There's no point."

"That's not the attitude, Mrs Davies. Your leg is healing and it seems you have good friends around you. I'm sorry to hear about your father but perhaps a change of scene is all you need. Is there anything I can do to make you feel better? Would you like to see the almoner?" He held her hand and she began to relax.

"You think talking things through with someone might help?"

"It's better than threatening to end it all."

"I'm sorry. I didn't mean it. I'm sorry I worried the physio."

"We don't like to see our patients depressed – we want you to leave here feeling positive."

"I'll try. Thank you, doctor," Valerie said. She was being selfish, she supposed. There were a lot of people worse off than she was. Perhaps she wanted too much. Perhaps she should just live each day as it comes and damp down her hopes and dreams. She still had to work out how to get up and down stairs on one good leg. Pete had fixed her banister but she knew she would feel uncertain for a while, especially in the house on her own. Anyway – she needed to be strong for her mother next week, and that should give her enough to focus on for the time being.

Chapter 25

The journey to Wales seemed to pass much more quickly than Valerie had expected. She told Joe more about her previous visit to the vineyard and that she had asked Fiona to tell Richard that she wanted to end their relationship.

"It wasn't easy," she said, "but we won a weekend away in a hotel and I can't go with him. I asked Fiona to try to match him with someone else."

"And did she?"

"I don't know, but then I broke my leg and I didn't want him coming to the hospital with flowers and making me feel even more indebted to him."

"Doesn't he know about your accident?"

"No. I've emailed him to tell him I'm going to Wales for the funeral. He's very busy. I don't think he'll expect to see me until I get back."

"You do like to keep secrets, don't you?"

"Not really. I just don't expect other people to be interested."

"Has having Bertie to talk to helped?"

"It's been a godsend. He stops me feeling absolutely alone. You don't think I'm stupid, do you, Joe?"

"Not at all. I think this is our turning. We're here, Valerie."

"And Christine is here to greet us. Thank goodness. I was getting stiff."

Valerie climbed out of the passenger seat and embraced her sister.

"Christine, this is Joe. He offered to bring me."

"Hallo, Joe. We've found you a van. It's not one of the newest ones, I'm afraid, but it's clean."

"Thanks, Christine. I'll go wherever I'm put. This place looks very pretty."

"Come and see Mum," Christine said to Valerie. "You're in the house with me, they've put a sofa bed in the spare room. Will you be able to manage on that? After that we can get Joe settled."

"It will probably be easier than a normal bed," Valerie replied. "I feel stronger every day."

"I'll wait here, shall I?" asked Joe.

"No, come in," Valerie replied. "I'll introduce you. There's no need to be shy with my family."

Joe was very quiet next morning when he joined them for breakfast. Taking Valerie to one side after the meal he said, "I won't come to the funeral, Valerie. I don't want people to get the wrong idea. After all, I'm only the taxi driver."

"Oh, I hadn't thought.." Valerie stuttered. "I just sort of assumed you would."

"I know – but I'd rather just look around. I haven't been away from home in years and it's a lovely area. I'll see you tonight, when it's all over. Your family would prefer it, I'm sure."

"All right. It will stop people being curious, I suppose. At least one of us will have a pleasant day."

"I'm sorry-"

"No – don't say anything else. I understand." She felt foolish at not considering how it would look to others if he was accompanying her, but there wasn't time to dwell on his decision. Her family was what mattered now.

In fact Joe did not appear that evening until ten o'clock when he knocked on the door of the bungalow and hovered in the doorway.

"I just came to say goodnight. I'll see you in the

morning. I won't come in," he said when Valerie opened the door.

"OK. Breakfast is at eight," Valerie replied. "I expect you want to be on the road by nine."

"I haven't got a timetable. I'll be guided by you," Joe said. "I filled up yesterday so we won't have to stop for petrol."

"Right, goodnight, then, Joe."

"Goodnight, Valerie."

It was an embarrassed Valerie who went back into the living room after this exchange. She had not considered the cost to Joe of this trip.

"I'm such a fool," she told Christine. "I just took him for granted."

"But he's not a boyfriend?"

"No – it's never been like that. He's just a chum. We share an allotment."

"Maybe he'd like to share more?"

"Oh, stop it, Chrissie. You're making things more complicated. How do I get him to accept a contribution for the journey?"

"Well, he has had free bed and breakfast."

"I suppose so. I hadn't thought of that. Do you think he might have treated it as a mini holiday?"

"Possibly – then you shouldn't feel so bad."

"I wonder what he did all day yesterday?"

"Ask him."

"I will, on the way back. Thanks, Chrissie, you've made me feel better. How long are you staying?"

"Another week. Then I'll have to go home. Mum doesn't have long to decide what to do. She says she needs to see the summer season over before she thinks long term."

"I'll come back in the Spring. I should be off these

crutches and might have my own car by then."

"Great, Well, I'm glad today's over."

"Yes, I'll just say goodnight to Mum. Thanks again, Chris."

"No problem."

"How did you spend the day , yesterday Joe?" Valerie asked once they were well on their way.

"I just explored, "Joe replied. "I went down to the beach, I took the little path through the woods. I went into the village and had lunch in the pub. I took the car to the nearest garage and I took a lot of photographs. Your family's site has a lovely position."

"There's a lot of new houses in the area since I last came."

"It's quite a neat community, not as isolated as I imagined. There's even a strip of land that would make perfect allotments. Your gardener does a good job, although there's potential for improvement."

"You mean the layout of the place?"

"Yes, the paths and the drainage – but that's me with my work hat on!"

"You"ll need that for the vineyard."

"I suppose, but it will be very different."

He fell silent and Valerie closed her eyes for a moment. She felt tired, tired of putting on a brave face, tired of feeling life was passing her by and she would be middle aged before she had achieved anything. I mustn't be miserable, she told herself. I've so much to be grateful for, but she wasn't convinced. Coming away from Wales made her look at her life in a new way. It had been fine when she thought it was going to continue without change but now Joe had said he was moving to France she realised what a hole that would leave in her life. She had come to rely on the fact that he was always there. She had known that whenever she was feeling down just being with him would cheer her. The warmth she felt in his presence wasn't just from the tea and biscuits, it was also because she trusted that he was fond of her, that he liked being with her and she didn't know anyone who made her feel more relaxed and, perhaps, more loved.

Valerie woke as they pulled into a service station. "Lunch, I think," Joe declared. "Come on, sleepy head."

"We haven't drunk all the coffee," Valerie said.

"That will keep. I fancy a baguette and a sticky bun," he called out as he came round to her door.

"Oh, Joe, that's all too fattening."

"Do I care? Come on, I'll work it all off tomorrow," and he took her hand to help her out of the car and then walked ahead of her to open the door of the service station.

"How about we stop at the garden centre on the way home?" Joe asked. "We should be planning what to grow this year."

"Are you sure you'll be here to see it?" Valerie countered.

"Well, if I'm not here you'll have to work twice as hard, and you've got the hut."

Valerie blushed, remembering when she suspected him of hiding her stolen goods. She didn't want his hut. She would much rather he stayed but it had to be his decision.

"If you are going to have a vineyard I know someone who might be able to help," Valerie began. "There's a local wine grower who could give you some tips."

"Not if he saw us as competition," Joe laughed.

"But I'm not even sure it will ever happen."

"I'll treat you to tea, then," she said. "I must do something to thank you for this trip."

"Fine, you sit here and I'll fetch whatever you want," he laughed, standing her crutches against the wall.

"I know I've been asleep half the journey but I'm really tired, Joe," Valerie confessed. "Here's ten pounds. I'll just have soup and a roll."

"Any sort?"

"Whatever. Mushroom's my favourite."

She turned to sit at the empty table and bumped into a man walking past her. Looking up she realised he was familiar, very familiar. It was Richard and he had a dangerous expression on his face.

"You didn't take long," he hissed.

"It isn't what it looks like."

"It looks pretty cosy to me."

Joe turned away from the counter, a number in his hand, but not for long.

Richard pushed Valerie out of the way and landed a punch on Joe's face, sending him staggering backwards as the little sign clattered to the floor.

"Richard, remember who you are," Valerie said as she tried to catch hold of his free arm. His almost purple face turned towards her and he gasped for air.

"Get away, quick," she said and pushed past him to get to Joe who was sitting in a pile of knives and forks that he had knocked from the table. He had his hand up to his face and gave a low moan. Valerie put her hand on the table and tried to crouch down beside him. "Joe, I'm so sorry," she said. "Can you stand up?"

An assistant came from behind the counter with a first aid kit. One or two customers had risen from their chairs to witness the occurrence. Valerie hoped they hadn't taken any photographs.

"It's all right, folks," she called out. "It's just a misunderstanding," and she looked round for Richard. He was nowhere to be seen.

Joe was ushered to a chair and given a cold sponge to hold to his eye,

"Can you see all right?" Valerie asked, collapsing into the chair beside him.

"I think so. Who was that? Why did he hit me?"

"It was Richard. He's got a temper. He just got the wrong end of the stick."

Joe winced as he tried to smile. "I should say. I feel it was me that got the stick!"

"Did anyone see what happened?" asked the assistant. "That was assault."

"The chap's gone," replied a customer. "Anyone got a photo?" but nobody had.

"I think we'll have our tea, now," Valerie said. "Thanks, everyone."

Joe took the sponge away from his eye. "It's OK. Only bruised. I'll live," he said. "You do have the oddest friends."

"Shh- "Valerie said. "We didn't know who it was, did we?"

"Oh, I see. No, it must have been a case of mistaken identity."

It was a very subdued Valerie who went to bed that night. A pleasant journey had been ruined by her ex boyfriend. Should she have protected him? She knew how proud he was to be a police inspector but should he be in that position if he couldn't control his temper?

She would have to contact him sometime, if he

didn't call her first. Wasn't there something called 'anger management?' She didn't want to be the reason he lost his job.

Chapter 26

Meanwhile she had to try to make it up to Joe. He'd been so entranced with her caravan site that it made her wonder if perhaps the answer to her lifestyle choices lay in Wales. After all, she had the business skills to help her mother with the site. If, as seemed a reasonable idea from her researches suggested, they limit it to residential homes so that the extra work involved in the holiday side was reduced, it could be a steady source of income.

All she would need is someone with the vision and energy to upgrade the site and she thought she knew just the person.

Her head was still full of plans for the park home site when Fiona phoned to give her some unexpected news.

"Richard came in yesterday," she said. "He wanted to tell me to take him off our books."

"Oh, dear. Was he very upset?"

"Not at all. What did he have to be upset about?"

"He was quite angry when he saw me with someone else. I hope you warned everyone about his jealousy."

"I warned Stephanie. She's the actress I told you about. They met a few days ago and something clicked. I think it was 'lust at first sight' but both of them have thanked me for the introduction. Richard looked a different man."

"I suppose she's going on the weekend away, now."

"I think so. She's very excited."

"I hope it works out. Richard did seem rather needy."

"I think she's right for him, as long as he doesn't mind her job. That could cause a problem if he sees her playing a romantic lead."

"I bet he likes showing her off."

"Yes, she's a bit of a blonde bombshell – but she's got her head screwed on. He might be a police inspector but I feel she'll be the one wearing the trousers."

Valerie giggled. At least one of the men in her life was settled, she thought. Was it possible that she could do the same for the other one?

Her heart was thumping as she returned to the allotment that weekend. She hoped Joe's black eye did not mean he was not going to appear, but he did, looking his usual shambolic self. Could it be that they both wanted the same thing? She'd never tried to analyse how she felt about him but now she was about to lose him it had become clearer. She didn't want to have a life without him in it.

First, she had to make sure his heart wasn't in France with Laurence.

Valerie was looking along a row of lettuces, pushing them gently with the end of her crutch to see if there were any slugs and snails when Joe arrived with a bag of compost.

She straightened up and looked at him, suddenly fearful of his reaction to her ideas.

"Hallo, Joe. I've been thinking about our partnership. I don't think I can carry on alone if you go abroad."

"So have I," said Joe. "I've told Laurence I'm not joining him. It was just a pipe dream. He needed to have a partner who knew what they were doing with vines. It's not really my thing. Why don't you come

155

and have a cuppa when you're done?"

Valerie leant on her crutches, steadying herself as she moved along the path, trying to make sure they didn't sink into the mud.

The little wooden hut seemed like a sanctuary, somehow, and she sat on the bench, sighed and dipped a ginger biscuit in her tea.

"We make a good team, don't we?" Joe began, smiling at her.

"That's what I was thinking. How would you like to help run the park home site?"

Joe's eyebrows shot up and he took a deep breath.

"Are you really considering it?"

"If I could find the right partner."

Joe paused, as if he was absorbing the message in her words. His brow furrowed as he asked,

"This looking for someone – has it worked out?"

"Not very well."

"Did you consider looking nearer home?"

"Not until this week."

"And now what?"

"Would you like to come for a meal?"

"At your place?"

"Yes."

"I'd be delighted and I'll be able to check on Bertie."

Valerie let out a breath that she hadn't been aware she was holding in. Was he teasing her?

"He's fine. He's grown about three feet since you gave him to me."

"I knew you'd look after him."

"He might be just a rubber plant but he filled a hole in my life. He's my Jiminy Cricket. I talk to him, you know."

Joe laughed. "And does he talk back?"

"It feels like it. He helps me get my ideas sorted in my head. He gave me the idea of inviting you to dinner."

"I see- and what does he think of the idea of us both moving to Wales?"

"He says it's a perfect solution to my problem. Oh, Joe, I've been a silly sausage."

"No, my dear. You just needed time. I've waited for this moment for so long."

He reached out to her and his embrace seemed so natural. She smiled up at him, warmed by the love in his eyes and comforted by the realisation that she had made the right choice, at last.

Julie C Round

Julie C Round was born in January 1942 in Slough and spent her formative years in Ealing. She then trained as a teacher at Balls Park College near Hertford and began her career in London.

While there she met her future husband and they were married in Worthing, Sussex. They then moved to the North East where their first son was born. Work commitments saw the family move south to Gillingham, in Kent and then near Sevenoaks.

While in Gillingham Julie was a County Councillor for four years but returned to the world of Education by retraining as a tutor for dyslexics.

With both sons married and living away the next move was back to Worthing where she began to write short stories, followed by self published novels. Her interest in social issues became apparent as she included prejudice, abandonment and crime in what are essentially stories of personal development.

Her recent activities include writing a pantomime and recording for the Sussex Coast Talking Newspaper.

She is an enthusiastic listener to traditional jazz and folk music and gives talks to the WI and other groups about her life and books.

Works

Julie began writing novels when her mother was widowed and her first book, 'Lane's End,' was written to entertain her.

This was followed by 'Un-Stable Lane' where the house the family are living in is flooded and 'The Third Lane,' where the daughter of the family has an accident and discovers more about the man she is due to marry than she would like.

All three books are about a man with learning difficulties and his family who live on the South Downs.

Her later novels,'Never Run Away' and 'Never Pretend' are also set in the Worthing area. These two books are about a married woman who tries to start a new life without her husband but finds it more difficult than expected, and the consequences of childhood trauma when faced with the issue of adoption.

In 2017 she published, 'A Lesson for the Teacher,' a love story set in the 1960's where three newly qualified schoolteachers find living and loving in the real world full of dangers and disappointments.

'A Bend in the Lane' a cautionary tale about an elderly widow who meets a charming gentleman while on holiday was published in 2019.

More about Julie and her books can be found on her website www.juliecround.co.uk or her blog www.juliecroundblog.wordpress.com.